WAITING FOR *Willa*

A BIG SKY NOVEL

NEW YORK TIMES BEST SELLING AUTHOR

KRISTEN PROBY

WAITING FOR WILLA

A Big Sky Novel

Kristen Proby

Copyright © 2019 by Kristen Proby

Cover Art:Photography by: Sara Eirew Photographer

Cover and Formatting Design: Uplifting Designs

ISBN: 978-1-63350-041-9

&
AMPERSAND
PUBLISHING, INC.

For Kirby

Other Books by Kristen Proby

The Big Sky Series

Charming Hannah
Kissing Jenna
Waiting for Willa

The Fusion Series

Listen To Me
Close To You
Blush For Me
The Beauty of Us
Savor You

The Boudreaux Series

Easy Love
Easy Charm
Easy Melody
Easy Kisses
Easy Magic
Easy Fortune
Easy Nights

The With Me In Seattle Series

Come Away With Me
Under the Mistletoe With Me
Fight With Me
Play With Me

Rock With Me
Safe With Me
Tied With Me
Breathe With Me
Forever With Me
Stay With Me
Indulge With Me
Love With Me

The Love Under the Big Sky Series

Loving Cara
Seducing Lauren
Falling For Jillian
Saving Grace

From 1001 Dark Nights

Easy With You
Easy For Keeps
No Reservations
Wonder With Me - Coming Soon

The Romancing Manhattan Series

All the Way
All it Takes

WAITING
FOR *Willa*
A BIG SKY NOVEL

PROLOGUE

Eight Years Ago...

Willa

IT DIDN'T KILL ME.

The worst possible thing that can happen to a person has happened to me, and I'm only twenty-two years old.

I don't feel the bitter Montana cold. I don't hear the words the minister whose name I only learned yesterday is saying. I'm numb, staring straight ahead at the rich mahogany that I insisted on.

If he's going to be in there for the rest of eternity, I want it to be nice, even if I can't afford it.

I'll figure it out.

My mom asked me last night why we didn't have life insurance, and I just laughed. For Christ's sake, Debbie, what twenty-two-year-olds do you know with life insurance?

I feel my lips tip up now at the thought, still

staring at the gleaming wood in the sunlight, and hear, "Amen."

There's shuffling around me. I'm hugged, patted, and people make sympathetic noises.

I don't care.

"Willa."

I've been talked around for the past four days. I scowl as I walk to the casket and lay my hand on the cold wood. How is it possible that just four days ago he was here? Warm and whole, his strong arms wrapped around me, and now he's just...*gone*.

I'm a widow at twenty-two.

"Willa."

It's louder this time, which means I'm required to answer. I glance around, surprised to find that aside from Max Hull, I'm alone. Cars pull away, and the cemetery workers huddle about thirty yards away, trying to stay warm.

"Hey," Max says as he moves closer to me, but I shake my head, warning him to stay back. Max knows me well, maybe better than anyone besides Cary, but Cary's gone now, so Max knows me the best, and he understands that I can't be touched. He holds his hands up in surrender. "Willa, I just wanted to say—"

"I don't care," I interrupt him and turn my eyes back to Cary's casket. The flowers on top are red roses. The baby in my belly kicks and I rub my hand over the spot, reminded that I have to pull it together for this little one.

"I'm sorry," he says, but I shake my head.

"Go away, Max."

"Willa."

I sigh and turn to look at him. God, he's handsome. He's the most handsome boy I've ever known.

And he left me without looking back. Left Cary, his best friend in the world.

"You've never been good at listening to me, Max, so I'm going to make this crystal-clear. I don't give a shit that you're sorry. You took him skiing, and you let him fall in that tree well. If you hadn't come to town *five years* after leaving it, my husband would be alive right now. So, no, I don't want to hear it. Go away." I push my finger into his chest, driving my point home. "I don't want anything to do with you."

He clenches his jaw, and his nostrils flare, but he doesn't argue. He just nods once, turns on his heel, and walks away, and I'm finally alone with my husband.

"I'm so damn mad," I whisper, shaking my head and looking back at the expensive wood, the flowers, and the photo of my man sitting in front. "I'm *pissed* at you, Cary Monroe. You told me you'd never leave."

For the first time since the phone call I never thought I'd receive, I feel tears threaten, and I give in to them.

"Everyone leaves," I mutter as the first drop

splashes down my cheek. "First Grandpa, then Max." I swipe at my wet face. "Then Daddy. But *you* were always there, holding my hand. Smiling. 'It's gonna be okay, Wills,' you said. 'I'm not going anywhere.'"

I sniff and shake my head.

"You fucking lied to me, Cary. And I'm so *mad* at you. I would open this expensive-as-hell casket and slap your face if I could."

I eye it, considering it.

"You know what I hate the most? That when Max picked you up that morning, I was irritated with you then, too. Because I wanted you to stay home and put the crib together, and you said you'd do it that afternoon. You'd have Max help."

A sob escapes.

"But now, you won't do that. And our son won't ever know you." I rub my belly again, comforted by the movement of the tiny child in my womb. "He won't know how funny you were, or how good it feels when you hold him."

I swallow hard and take a deep breath, trying to get myself under control.

"Actually, that's not true. He'll know you because I'll tell him about you. But it won't be the same." I lay my hand on the casket again. "It won't be the same at all. How am I supposed to do this without you?"

CHAPTER ONE

Willa

"**M**OM!" ALEXANDER CARY MONROE the love and light of my life, squirms in excitement as I try to get his shirt buttoned up. Winter means it's time for flannel, and flannel has buttons, and my eight-year-old doesn't stand still for long. "Mom. Mom. Mom."

"I'm changing my name," I inform him and wrestle him around so his back is pressed to my front. I quickly fasten the last three buttons. "My name is now officially, Penelope."

"Whatever, Mom," he says with a giggle. "I need to have a serious conversation with you."

"Then stop trying to get away from me. We have to leave in three minutes, and you don't have socks *or* shoes on."

My cell phone rings, and I blow out a breath of defeat.

"It's Nana!" he exclaims, accepting the call. "Hi, Nana. Yeah, I'm ready for school."

"Little liar," I mumble as I sweep spilled cereal into my hand and throw it in the trash, then quickly wipe down the countertop and grab my purse. "Socks and shoes, Alex."

"I know, I'm excited for the weekend, too. I get to go to Miss Hannah's wedding as Mom's date. Yep. I got a new suit and everything. Uh-huh. Okay, here's Mom. Love you, too."

"Socks and shoes, Alexander," I instruct him, taking the phone. "Hi, Jean."

"Hello, darling. I know it's always hectic in the morning, but I wanted to chat with Alex before the weekend got underway."

"You never have to apologize for calling," I reply with a smile. Cary's parents, Jean and Dan, have been so good to me over the past decade. They invited me into their family with open arms when I married their son, and they've been an important part of both Alex's and my life since Cary passed. We couldn't love them more. "Is everything okay?"

"Oh, yes, we're fit as fiddles."

"How is Arizona?"

"Not as cold as Montana," Jean says with a laugh, and I mouth *"let's go"* to Alex. "Anyway, I love you guys. I was just checking in."

"We love you too, Nana," I reply and toss my purse in the backseat next to Alex. "I'll be sure to call Sunday evening."

"Bye, Willa."

"Bye." I hang up and hurry into the car, make sure Alex is buckled up, and pull away from the house. I still live in the home that Cary and I bought when we found out that I was pregnant with Alex. I love it, but it's a good fifteen minutes from town, and I usually take my son to school rather than put him on the bus. It's extra time to chat with him in the mornings.

He's clearly a morning person.

"Mom! My birthday is only two weeks away."

"I know. I was there."

"I have a list of things I want, but there's really only one thing I need."

I cock an eyebrow and look at him in the rearview. His brown hair, which I combed only twenty minutes ago, is already sticking up on the side. His dimples are deep as he smiles, and his brown eyes are full of joy.

"What do you need?"

"A puppy."

I smirk and pull onto the highway toward town.

"Just hear me out, Mom," he says. "I'm very responsible."

"Says the kid who I have to wrestle into clothes five minutes before we leave the house."

"I like my pajamas," he says with a shrug. "But other than that, I'm responsible. I do my chores, and I clean my bedroom when you tell me to."

"You do those things," I agree.

"So, I'd be the perfect person to have a dog," he says, his voice pleading. "I'll make sure he goes outside, and you won't have to clean up after him or feed him or *anything*."

Right. And if I believe that, I'm sure there's some ocean-front property in Idaho I can invest in.

"A dog is a huge commitment," I remind him for the third time this week. Not because I'm trying to talk him out of it. No, I've already got the puppy picked out, and we will take a special trip on his birthday to pick it up. "If we get one, it will be part of our family for a *very* long time, Alex. You can't just decide that you've lost interest and move on to something else."

"I would never do that, Mom," he says, his voice serious. "A dog is a person that loves you no matter what. And we could train him to go with us to the shop."

"I don't want dog hair on the merchandise," I inform him, not willing to budge on this.

"I can do this. I can be a good dog owner. And, my birthday is the perfect time."

"We'll see. I haven't decided what you're getting for your birthday. I almost forgot it was coming."

I glance back to see him roll his eyes. "Whatever. You never forget anything."

I laugh as I turn into the drop-off line at school. "I love you, Bubba. Have a good day."

"Can I walk to the shop after school with Pierce?"

Pierce is Alex's new best friend, and he walks home from school.

"Yes, but you come *straight* to the shop, you hear me?"

"Yes, ma'am. Bye, Mom!"

He slams the car door shut, and I watch him hurry to the teacher standing by the entrance, then gasp when I see that he's wearing one white and one yellow sock.

"At least he's wearing socks," I mutter as I wave and pull away. "Mother of the year, right here."

The school is only about four blocks from downtown Cunningham Falls so he won't have far to walk. I love my town. I was born and raised here, and I always wanted to stay. A glamorous life in some city somewhere was never my dream.

That was Max Hull's dream, and that's why it never worked out between us.

I wanted to be here, in our sleepy town, with a husband and babies. I wanted a business. I wanted to be part of the PTA, the booster club, and I wanted to spearhead charity drives for the food bank.

And I have and do all of those things, minus the husband.

I pull into my parking space behind my store off the alley then gather my purse, coffee mug, and laptop, and make my way inside, disabling the alarm with just my pinky.

I'm a mom. Performing tasks with my hands full is my superpower.

I have two hours before I open, so I head up to my office and get busy taking inventory of the merchandise that was delivered yesterday, putting it on hangers and racks, ready for steaming.

I'll have Krista, my part-time help, steam the new clothes when she gets here this afternoon.

Before I know it, my phone pings, alerting me that I'm only five minutes from opening time. So, I grab my mug of now-cold coffee and head downstairs. Once the door is unlocked, and the *Open* sign is lit, I pop a pod into the Keurig at the coffee station behind the lingerie and brew a fresh cup.

Much to my surprise, Cary *did* have a life insurance policy. Apparently, he took it out after we found out that I was pregnant, and I've been diligent about where I've allocated the money. I socked some away for Alex's college, made a lot of repairs and upgrades to our house, and I took a year off of work when my little Alex came so I could get my feet under me.

Finally, about six months ago, I opened my own dress shop after working for someone else for way too long. *Dress It Up* is the other half of my heart. I carry smart, sexy, and beautiful clothes. Trendy pieces. Shoes that satisfy even the most discerning customer. And, yes, I serve coffee, wine in the evening, and when I'm feeling extra sassy, champagne.

"Willa," my best friend, Jenna, calls from the front of the shop. "Where are you?"

"Getting coffee," I call out. "Want one?"

"No, thanks."

I weave my way through the racks and meet Jenna at the checkout counter in the middle of the store. "Hey. You look...frazzled."

"Crazy morning," I reply and take a sip of coffee. "Alex was trying my patience."

"I think it's his official job to do that," she says with a smile. Jenna Hull is one of the sweetest people I know, and I've known her most of my life. Despite the history I have with her older brother, we have never let that get in the way of our love for each other.

She's also maybe the most gorgeous woman in the world, with classic Grace Kelly beauty. Blond hair. Blue eyes. Killer figure.

If I didn't love her so much, I'd hate her.

And when she takes a drink from her to-go cup from Drips & Sips, her engagement ring sparkles.

"How's Christian?" I ask, still stunned that my best friend is engaged to the hottest actor on the planet.

"He's amazing," she says with a grin. "He has business calls this morning, and I am running some errands for Hannah. I can't believe the wedding is this Saturday already."

"Time flies," I agree. "Is there anything I can do today? With the holidays over, I haven't been as slammed in here."

"I don't think so, but I'll keep you posted," she says with a sigh. "My big brother is getting married."

Brad Hull is the oldest sibling and the chief of police in Cunningham Falls. He fell head over heels for Hannah, an OBGYN who moved to town about five years ago. The man adores her, and I can't wait to see them get married on Saturday. I was honored when Hannah asked me to be one of her bridesmaids, along with Jenna, and Hannah's cousin, Abby.

"There are about twenty RSVPs out there in the universe that never made their way back," Jenna says with a sigh. "Why don't people just send back the damn card? It even has a stamp on it!"

"Because they're mysterious," I reply with a wink. "And if they're local, I'd plan on them being there. This wedding is a big deal."

"I think I'll just elope," she says with a sigh, and I feel my eyes widen in surprise.

"Really?"

"Nah, I need a pretty dress, but I'm in no hurry. And it won't be big like this. Christian doesn't need the media circus. I think we'll do something super small out at the property in the park."

"That would be amazing," I reply with a nod. "And I'd better be a part of that something small."

"Wouldn't have it any other way," she says with a smile. "I guess I should get over to Brooke's Blooms. I want to see the flowers in person."

"Sounds like fun. Say hi to Brooke for me, and call if you need anything."

"Will do."

***

"Introducing Mr. and Mrs. Brad Hull!"

The room erupts in applause as Brad and Hannah walk into the reception area of the Lodge on the mountain, hand in hand, huge smiles on their faces.

So full of hope and excitement.

I swipe a tear from my cheek and clap my hands, my feet screaming in my four-inch heels.

"Are you sad?" Alex asks beside me. He's in a black suit with a blush-colored tie that matches my dress because he's my date.

"No, sweetheart, I'm happy." I lean down to kiss his cheek, and he actually lets me, which doesn't happen often in public these days. "Sometimes, people cry because they're happy."

"Girls are weird," he says with a shrug.

"Girls aren't the only ones who cry when they're happy," I argue with a laugh. "Isn't Miss Hannah pretty?"

"I like her dress," he says. "It's not too poofy like on that show on TV."

"No, it fits her perfectly."

Hannah's red hair is pulled back into a simple twist, showing off the strapless dress, sweetheart neckline, and crystals that wink in the lights. Brad hasn't taken his hands off her since she walked down the aisle to him.

"Now it's time for the bridal party to dance," Jenna says into the MC's mic. "Come on, guys!"

The next thing I know, I'm coupled up with Max, and for the first time in more than a decade, I'm in his arms, dancing to a slow song by the Goo Goo Dolls.

"Hey," Max says with a half-smile. His arms are stiff around me, and his jaw is tight as if he'd rather be anywhere but here.

"Hi," I reply softly.

I used to love this man when we were so young that I thought we'd be together forever. But that wasn't to be. We wanted very different things.

Besides, not many people marry their childhood sweethearts these days.

Max and I have a long history. Some of it was wonderful, and some were the hardest times of my life.

But he's living here now, and I refuse to let things stay awkward between us. We have the same friends, we move in the same circles.

I need to extend an olive branch.

"You know, it's not fair," I begin.

"What's that?" he asks, cocking an eyebrow.

"That we're all aging, but you just get better looking."

His jaw stops, clenching as he takes a deep breath and finally smiles down at me with that grin that used to melt me into a puddle at his feet.

"Is that so?"

"I'm not telling you anything you don't know," I reply with a shrug. "You and Christian were both in that magazine a few months ago."

"You read it?" he asks.

"I'm a woman over the age of sixteen," I remind him. "Of course, I read it."

"Tell me more about how you think I'm better looking."

I laugh now, leaning in to rest my forehead on his chest and discreetly clenching my legs so I don't pee myself.

Having a baby will do things to your body, like make your bladder weaker than a newborn bunny.

"You always were humble," I say when I can breathe again.

"You started it."

"So I did."

"How are you, Willa?"

"I'm great," I reply honestly. "How are you?"

"I can't complain," he says. He looks like he wants to say more, but suddenly, my son is tapping my arm.

"Mom, I want to dance, too."

"Okay, Bubba. Alex, do you remember Mr. Max?"

"Hi, Alex," Max says, smiling down at my son.

"Hi. Sorry to interrupt, but Mom said she'd dance with me."

"She's all yours," Max says, passing my hand over to Alex and nodding. "See you around, Wills."

Wills.

Only Max and Cary called me Wills. I haven't heard that out loud in almost nine years.

"Mom."

I glance down. "Yes, baby?"

"I have moves."

I chuckle and rest my hand on his shoulder, letting him guide me over the floor. "Yes, you do."

***

"I'm not tired," Alex says with a yawn. He can't keep his eyes open as I tug the covers up to his chin.

"Well, I am," I reply and kiss his cheek. "Did you have fun tonight?"

"Yeah. I danced with all the girls."

"Yes, you did." I kiss him again. "You're quite the charmer, aren't you?"

"Like Dad?"

I sigh, breathing him in. His baby smell is long gone, replaced tonight by the scent of soap from his shower after we got home. He's soft and cozy, and there are still brief moments like this one when he's sleepy and tucked into bed, that he's my baby.

"Yes, your dad was a charmer."

"Tell me," he says, settling in. This is a story I've told him since he was born. I don't tell it as often now, but sometimes, when he's not feeling well or has been thinking about his dad, he'll ask for it.

And I always comply because I promised Cary that his son would know him.

"Your dad was born right here in Cunningham Falls, on March sixteenth," I begin, lying next to him and holding him to me. "And just like you, he was a wonderful boy. I met him in Kindergarten. We had Mrs. Wilhem, in the morning class…"

CHAPTER TWO

Max

"COME ON, MAN. IT'LL be a rush," Cary says as he adjusts his goggles on his face.

"It hasn't been groomed," I insist, looking down the backside of the mountain. We got a lot of fresh snow last night, and I'm worried. This could be dangerous. "Don't be stupid."

"Don't be a pussy," he throws back at me, smiles, then pushes off, gaining speed quickly.

My skis are stuck in the snow. I'm pushing with my poles, and it's like moving through mucky water. I can't pick up speed.

"Come on!" he yells.

"Stop!" I scream back, but he can't hear me. And I can't make my goddamn feet move.

I'm sweating, breathing hard, and watching the blue ski jacket make its way farther and farther *down the mountain until it just...disappears.*

"No!" Suddenly, I'm propelled down, my feet unstuck, and I'm going too fast. I'm going to whiz right past where I last saw Cary.

But when I zoom close, I get stuck again and fall down. Cary's buried in the snow, but his face is showing, staring up at me.

"Should have stopped me, man," he says.

"No." I try to crawl to him, but I'm stuck in the snow again. "No, no, no, no, no."

Right before my eyes, Cary sinks into the tree well, slowly as if he's in quicksand, and disappears completely.

I can't reach him.

I can't save him.

"Fuck!"

I jolt up in bed, sweating and panting. I've kicked the covers to the floor, and I'm wrapped from the waist down in the sheet, making my legs immobile.

"Fuck," I say again and rest my elbows on my knees, my head in my hands as I try to catch my breath.

I haven't dreamed about that day in a while, but it shouldn't surprise me that I am now. Seeing Willa at the wedding tonight was bound to bring it up.

It always does, even when I don't talk to her.

In fact, tonight was the first time I've spoken to

her in nine years.

I sigh, pushing my hands through my hair, and climb out of bed. I won't sleep again tonight, so I might as well get some work done.

I pull on some shorts and walk down to the kitchen to get a cup of coffee. Black.

Then I wander into my office. Rather than sit down at my desk, I walk to the wall of windows that look out to the lake.

It's dark, but the moon is full and bright, glistening off the water. It's a calm, clear winter night. For the first time that I can remember, the lake hasn't frozen over all the way, just around the edges.

Cary and I used to love to cross-country ski across the lake when we were kids. We got a kick out of the fact that we were walking over the fish.

God, I missed Willa and Cary after I left. More than I missed my family, although I missed them, too.

But I was determined to make something of myself outside of Montana. I was tired of the small-town existence. I wanted to live in a city, go to college, and experience life.

I *needed* it.

I wanted Willa to go with me, but she didn't see herself living anywhere but here in Cunningham Falls. So, we broke up, and I went to college.

But I always intended to come back and talk her into going with me. I was convinced that she'd miss me and give in.

Yeah, I was a cocky little bastard.

That cockiness served me well in business.

Not so much in my love life.

And just when I was ready to say, "*fuck it*" and come home to her, I got a call from Cary. He'd asked her to marry him, and she'd said yes.

My best friend was going to marry my girl.

I almost felt betrayed, which is fucked up because I'm the one who left Willa behind. I was an asshole to think that she'd pine away for me, waiting until I came to swoop her up and carry her away.

And, if she was going to marry anyone else, at least it was a guy I loved and respected.

I wasn't happy. I wasn't content.

But I learned to live with it.

And just when I got up the fucking nerve to come home and see everyone after being away for far too long, Cary and I went skiing, and he fell into that tree well and died.

It happened in the blink of an eye, and he was gone.

Cary was gone, and Willa wanted nothing to do with me.

So, I left and made something of myself. I dove into work. It consumed me. No amount of success or respect or money mattered to me. It was never enough.

Until I came home for Christmas about five years ago and realized that this was where I was supposed to be all along.

I respected Willa's wishes, though. She told me at the cemetery that day that she wanted nothing to do with me, and I've stayed away, even though everything in me yearns for her. I've kept my distance.

Until tonight when I had her in my arms and heard her sweet voice, her laugh. Felt her body pressed against mine. God, she hasn't changed a bit.

And her son is the spitting image of his daddy.

I didn't want to leave them there on the dance floor, but I did. And I'll continue to stay away from her. Because what I want from Willa, she'll never give me.

I want everything. I want her *and* her son. I want her laughter, her sighs, and her tears. I want to give her everything I have, and I want to take care of her and Alex.

And I'm a grade-A asshole for it.

I shake my head and turn back toward my desk. Taking a sip of my lukewarm coffee, I sit down and start up all four computers. It's time to bury myself in work.

***

"Jesus, you could kill someone," Gray King says to

Christian. They're playing darts, and Christian has one hell of an arm.

"Don't stand in front of the board," Christian suggests, making us all laugh.

"Yellow, corner pocket," I say to Noah King before I tap the ball and send it into the target.

The guys are here for some beer and laid-back conversation. The only one missing is Brad, but he's on his honeymoon in the Caribbean. I invite everyone over about once a month.

"How's the bird rescue business?" I ask Noah as I rub blue chalk on the end of my cue.

"Steady," he says, studying the balls on the table. "I had a barn owl brought in today. Someone shot it with a .22 and left it for dead."

"People are assholes," Gray says in disgust.

"I won't disagree with you," Noah replies. "How's the billionaire life?"

My lips twitch. Gray and Noah have known me since we were kids. We all grew up together. And they never get tired of flipping me shit for being rich.

"Oh, you know. I bought a new yacht yesterday."

"Seriously?" Gray asks. "Because if you did, I'm borrowing it."

"No, but I looked at one online. It could be a good investment."

"Don't do it," Christian says, surprising me. "I

have a friend who did, and it was a pain in the ass more than a good time."

"Good to know," I reply, leaning on my cue as Noah takes his turn on the table.

"If it impresses the ladies, I say do it," Gray says with a grin.

"Speaking of ladies to impress," Noah says, "did you guys see Willa at the wedding the other night?"

And just like that, every nerve on my body is on high alert.

I take a pull off my beer, keeping my face neutral, but my hands clench on the pool cue.

"She's hot," Gray agrees with a nod and then throws a dart. "That dress showed off her ass nicely."

I want to tear him limb from limb for even having the audacity to *look* at her ass.

"I might ask her out," Noah replies thoughtfully, and I react without thinking.

"Fuck, no," I say, my voice a growl.

"No?" Noah asks, rubbing his chin. "Why's that?"

"Just no," I repeat and toss my empty bottle into the trash, then open the fridge for another.

"Last I checked, you're not her daddy, and she's a grown woman so I can ask her out if I damn well please," Noah says. Both Gray and Christian have stopped their game and watch us with interest.

"You know there's history there," I reply.

"Ancient history," he says. "You dated her in high school, man. So, what? You dated her, so she can't date anyone else in this town? Is she supposed to die an old maid? You didn't brand her, Max."

"Don't be an asshole," I reply calmly but feel anything *but* calm.

"I'm a man, and Willa's an attractive woman. So unless you're going to ask her out yourself, I don't think there's much you can say here."

I narrow my eyes at him, pissed as hell, but he's right.

I don't have a claim on Willa.

And that pisses me off, too.

"He's still in love with her," Gray says quietly.

"Then maybe he should do something about it," Noah says, his arms crossed over his chest, watching me defiantly. "Shit, or get off the pot."

"I don't think we should equate Willa to a pot," Christian says. "It's just gross."

"You know what I mean," Noah says.

"You started this on purpose," I reply and watch as a smile spreads over my friend's face.

"We saw you at the wedding," Gray says. "We saw the way you looked at her when you were dancing with her."

"How's that?" I ask, then hate myself for it because I probably don't want to know.

"Like she hung the damn moon," Christian says, then shrugs when I stare at him. "Jenna's told me a lot about your past with Willa, and I watch. Jenna said it was a big deal that you danced with her."

"He doesn't usually go near her," Gray confirms, and I scowl.

"Are y'all just sitting around, talking about my non-existent love life like a bunch of gossiping women?" I toss my cue on the table and march to the doors that open to the balcony that overlooks the lake. I step out into the snow and take a deep breath of the crisp air.

"If she's what you want, you should do something about it," Noah says from behind me, and I turn to find all three men standing on the balcony with me. "Because if you don't, someone else will."

The pain that the thought of someone else touching Willa brings me is a hell that I wouldn't wish on an enemy.

"Maybe I'm not what she needs," I reply. "She made it clear a long time ago that she doesn't want anything to do with me."

"She was young and hurt," Gray says. "Hell, we all were. And, yeah, she might tell you to go fuck yourself. But at least you'd have tried."

"Why do I feel like this was an intervention?" I ask, propping my hands on my hips.

"No idea," Gray says with a smile. "We just

came over to drink your beer and beat you at pool."

"Maybe the kid is the problem," Noah says thoughtfully. "Are you hanging back because you don't want to take on another man's child?"

"That's a shitty thing to say," I reply. "Alex is a great kid."

"Some men wouldn't want to take on the baggage of someone else's family."

"Some men are assholes," Christian says with a sigh. "Max isn't."

"No, I'm not," I agree. "It's not the kid."

"Do something," Noah repeats. "But first, let's start that pool game over so I can kick your ass."

"You can try." I follow my friends back inside and watch as Noah sets up the balls to break them. Maybe he's right. I've wasted a lot of time hanging back and steering clear of Willa because I thought it was what she wanted.

Maybe it's time I let her go altogether.

***

I've been here since before the sun came up. I'm sitting in a camping chair I brought with me with a six-pack of beer next to my feet, keeping cold in the snow. I pop the top of the second one in an hour and reach out to clink the neck of the bottle against the one on the headstone.

"Nine years," I say, blowing out a breath. I come here every year on the anniversary of Cary's death and just sit here, hanging out with him. I drink two beers, leave the rest for him, and then go home to finish getting drunk alone.

The cemetery sits on the edge of town. It's pretty much full now, all of the plots either housing someone or sold. Cary sits up on the hill, closest to the railroad tracks, and looks out over the lake and Blacktail Mountain.

It's cold this morning. A painful twenty-two degrees to be exact, but I don't care. I'm bundled up.

The alcohol helps.

"Time flies," I mutter, shaking my head as I watch a train speed by. The whistle pierces the air. "Jesus, I still *feel* twenty-three. I don't look it." I shrug. "I wonder if you would have had grey hair by now like your dad did at thirty."

I clear my throat.

"I've managed to keep the grey hair at bay, but I'm told that having salt and pepper hair is distinguishing, so I guess it won't be so bad.

"You know what sucks? I need woman advice, and I can't ask you. Of course, if you were here, I wouldn't be asking because it's about Willa, and that makes me feel like a dick. Like I'm poaching on my best friend's wife, even though I know that's not the case. And you poached first. Let's just establish that right now."

The whistle blows again, making me smile.

"Yeah, I know. She's irresistible. I don't know what to do, Cary. Part of me thinks I should just keep my distance. Let her go."

I take another swig of beer.

"And the shitty thing is, I'm still so drawn to her, you know?"

I stare at the headstone, reading it over and over again.

Cary Edward Monroe

1987-2010

Loving Son, Husband, and Friend

"So, if you could just let me know that you're not pissed at me for even considering starting something with her, I'd appreciate it."

I wait, but there's nothing. Just silence.

"Does that mean you're *not* okay with it?"

Nothing.

"Okay, then. Brad got married about a week ago. He married a nice woman that moved here a few years ago. I like her a lot."

And so I spend the next hour, talking to my best friend in the cold, filling him in on my life, and the lives of everyone we know.

Just when I'm about to get up and leave, I hear footsteps behind me. I shift in my chair and glance back, surprised to see Willa standing there, her hands in her pockets and a bouquet of roses tucked under one arm.

"Hi."

CHAPTER THREE

Willa

"HE CAN HAVE CEREAL for breakfast, but don't let him talk you into hot chocolate as well," I inform my mom, who's currently snuggling with my sleepy son on the couch.

"I've been watching my grandson for almost nine years," she reminds me and kisses Alex's head. "We'll be fine."

"Right." I nod and rush to grab my purse and keys, but my keys aren't in their usual spot.

I frown, glancing around.

"Alex?"

"Yeah?"

"Have you seen my keys?"

I immediately curse under my breath as I stomp into the kitchen, bathroom, and my bedroom, looking around for them.

I *hate* today. Today is the worst day of the year. If I didn't have a little boy to see to, I'd spend it under the covers.

But I do have a son, and I'm stronger than that.

Or, at least I tell myself I am.

"You had them when you drove the car," Alex replies, making me smile. Why would I ask an almost nine-year-old if he's seen my keys?

And why can't I find them?

"Are they in your purse?" Mom asks.

I look through it, blowing out a breath when I don't find them.

"Nope. They're here somewhere." I open the fridge because I did that once before when I was super tired, and Alex had the flu. But they're not there. On a whim, I open the pantry, and...*score!* There they are. "Found them!"

"Where were they?"

"The pantry." I walk back into the living room as I pull on my coat. "I don't remember putting them there, but at least I found them."

"Are you okay?" Mom asks, and I know it's not about the keys.

"Yeah. I won't be long."

"Take all the time you need," she says.

"See you in a bit, Bubba."

"Bye, Mom."

"Oh!" I rush back, poking my head into the living room. "He had a shower last night, so—"

"Willa, my love," Mom interrupts me with a soft smile. "We're fine."

"Right." I nod. "Thanks. See you later."

I wave and walk out to my car in the garage. It's been giving me trouble lately. I should replace it, but I just paid the sucker off, and I'm determined to get through two years payment-free, so I'll make an appointment to have it checked out later this week.

The drive to town is uneventful. It's a cold Sunday morning. The roads are clear of snow and not busy at all. Most people are either at church or still in bed.

Where I'd like to be.

I don't know why I do this every year. Cary isn't in that casket. I often feel him around me, and I talk to him all the time. He's not *at* the cemetery.

Yet, I go. Every single year. I always take a bouquet of red roses. Some years, the snow is deep, and I have to uncover his headstone. But it's been a dry year. Cold, but without a lot of snow.

I park my car along the small drive about a block away from where Cary is, zip up my coat and grab my gloves, and head out, crunching through the snow between the headstones, and see someone already at Cary's grave.

It looks like he's talking. He's sitting in a red camping chair, bundled up in ski gear and a hat, but I'd know those shoulders anywhere.

Max.

I don't know why I'm surprised. Max was Cary's best friend and was with him when he died.

Of course, he misses him.

I don't want to startle him, but I also don't want to hang back and be a creeper, so I keep walking closer, my boots crunching the hard snow. Max turns.

"Hi," I say softly.

He raises a beer. "Come join us."

I cock a brow and walk closer, noticing the beer at Max's feet, and the open one on Cary's headstone.

"I always wondered who brought the beer," I say when I walk around Max and set the roses next to the brew. "I should have known."

"Want one?" he asks.

"Actually, that sounds good. It's five o'clock somewhere, right?"

"That it is," he says, pops the top on a bottle, and passes it to me. I take a swig, surprised that it feels good on my throat despite the bitter cold.

"Do you need a ride home?"

Max's lips twitch the way they always did when he was particularly amused by me.

"I only have two, then I leave the rest for him."

I nod and take a deep breath. "I've never minded the cold, you know."

He nods.

"I think it feels nice." I take another swig of beer and sit on the snow, leaning against Cary's headstone.

"I should leave you be," he says, moving to stand, but I hold up a hand.

"Wait." I clear my throat. "I have some things to say, and I think this is a good place to say them."

He stands, and I think he's going to leave anyway, which I wouldn't blame him for, but the next thing I know, he reaches for my hand, pulls me to my feet, and gestures for me to sit in his chair before sitting in my spot on the ground.

"You shouldn't sit on the ground, Wills," he says softly after settling on the snow. "What do you want to say?"

"That I'm sorry," I blurt and blink rapidly, making this up as I go because I didn't expect to see him here today. "I want to apologize for what I said to you that day."

"You don't need to."

"Yeah, I do." I nod and take a sip of beer. "I was angry, Max. Not just at you, but at Cary and, well, the universe. I took it out on you. It was like all of the grief and the pain just boiled up, and I spewed it all over you.

"It wasn't your fault that Cary died, Max. He was a thrill-seeker, especially when it came to skiing. He *loved* it. I can't even count how many times I told him to stop going out of bounds because it wasn't safe. He would just pat me on the head like I was being cute and do it anyway."

Max takes a deep breath, and I swear his shoulders sag as if a huge weight has been lifted off them. Jesus, has he been carrying that around all of these years because of me?

The thought of that tears a hole in my heart.

"You lost him, too. It took me a long time to see that I wasn't the only one who was grieving. I know that makes me selfish."

"No, it makes you human," he replies, and my gaze catches his for a long moment. My God, I loved him. Once upon a time, he was everything to me.

"I *was* incredibly angry with you," I admit and watch as his jaw tightens, but he doesn't drop his gaze from mine. "But my anger was layered."

"In what way?"

"You left me," I remind him. "And you didn't come back. You were my *life* for years, and suddenly, you were just gone. I was sure that something was wrong with me."

"No," he says adamantly, shaking his head.

"I was seventeen, Max. Of course, I thought it was *me*. You were gone, and Cary missed you, too. We definitely leaned on each other through that, and I fell in love with him, and we built a life together. But I never shook my anger for you. And then, you came back out of the blue, and, well, you know the rest."

"Your husband died on my watch," he finishes.

"Yeah. Men leave me, Max." I gasp, mortified that I said it out loud, but Max just narrows his eyes in curiosity.

"Keep going."

"Is this therapy with Cary?" I ask, hoping to change the subject.

"You said it was a good place for it," he reminds me. "Are you too cold?"

"No." I sniff, the chill in the air making my nose drip. "I was close to my gramps," I remind him. "And he died. Then you left. My daddy died a couple years later."

"I liked your dad very much," Max says.

"He liked you, too," I whisper. "Then Cary."

"I always planned to come back," Max admits, surprising me. "For you."

"What?"

"I thought that once I left for college, you'd miss me enough that when I came back for your graduation, I could talk you into leaving with me. I realize that was a stupid way of thinking."

"You didn't come back."

"When I spoke with Cary, he told me that he was dating you, and after you graduated, he asked you to marry him."

"I didn't know," I murmur, listening to the train whistle.

"Would it have changed anything?" he asks.

"I don't know," I reply honestly. "I still wouldn't have wanted to move away from Cunningham Falls, so, maybe not."

"I guess it's a waste of time to think about what-ifs."

"*If* it had changed things, I wouldn't have Alex, and I wouldn't wish him away for anything."

"He's a great kid. He looks just like Cary."

"I know." I smile, thinking about my handsome boy. "He even has some of the same mannerisms, which fascinates me because he never met Cary."

"I'm sorry," Max says, tears swimming in his brown eyes. "For all of it, Wills. Hurting you is the last thing I ever want to do."

"I know," I say and reach out to pat his shoulder. "I know that. And I've let go of a lot of the anger. I can't be a happy woman and raise a well-rounded son if I dwell on the bad things. I've had some therapy, and I am content with my life."

"I'm glad," Max says with a nod. "You've done a great job with your store. All of the women rave about it."

"Thank you. I love it. It's what I always wanted."

Except you, I think. I don't have Max. But I have *so much*.

"I'm really glad that I ran into you here," I say with a smile. "I needed to apologize, and I need for things to not be awkward between us. We have the same friends, and we move in the same circles."

"I was staying away from you because you told me that's what you wanted," he says with a shrug.

"Well, now we've cleared the air."

The train whistle blows once more.

"I've always thought the whistle was Cary talking to me."

Max's lips twitch. "Is that so?"

"Yeah. Stupid, isn't it?"

"No. No, it's not stupid."

***

"I'm cold," Alex says a few days later as we sit in my dead car on the side of the highway.

"I know, baby. I'm sorry. The tow truck should be here anytime."

"Why did the car die?" he asks.

Because the universe is out to get me today.

"I don't know. We'll have a mechanic look at it and fix it up."

He sits back in the seat, hugging his coat to him. It's dark outside, and I'm stranded on the side of the road with my almost-nine-year-old in a dead car. I don't think I've ever been as scared as when the vehicle lost power, but at least I was able to guide it off the road and avoid an accident.

"Maybe that's the tow truck," Alex says as someone pulls up behind us.

Wouldn't a tow truck pull up in front of me?

"Maybe," I murmur, watching in the mirror as the vehicle's lights cut off, and a man gets out of the SUV, walking to mine. "It's Max."

"He drives a tow truck?" Alex asks, excitement in his voice. Alex loves all vehicles. I swear, *he* might be a tow truck driver someday.

"No, he doesn't." Max knocks on my window, and I open the door. "Hi."

"What's going on?"

"It's dead. I'm waiting for the tow truck."

"Come sit in my car," he offers. "It's warmer."

I would decline, but my son is shivering, so I nod. "Thanks. Come on, buddy, Max is going to let us warm up in his car."

"Awesome," Alex says, immediately jumping out.

"Go get him," I say in a panic, and Max is already gone, taking Alex by the hand and leading him to the back of his Mercedes SUV. "Thanks," I say when I get in the passenger side.

"Wow!" Alex says, looking around the interior of the luxury SUV in awe. "Your car is super cool. Mom, look at all of the knobs!"

"I see them." I smile over at Max, who's just grinning at Alex's enthusiasm.

"This car is *way* better than ours. We should get one," Alex says, making me giggle with him.

"I think we'll just get our car fixed," I reply, not even wanting to *think* about how much the Mercedes costs. The boxy SUV is on my bucket list for when my store becomes a franchise.

A girl has to have goals.

Finally, the tow truck arrives, but when I move to climb out of the car, Max puts a hand on mine.

"You stay here and get warm. I can talk to him. Where do you want it towed?"

I give him the name of my mechanic, and he nods, then hops out and approaches the man. It's begun to snow, of course, making it more difficult to see.

I'm exhausted. It's been a long, long day. Alex came to the shop after school, and I had to help him with homework as I also assisted customers. My part-time help, Krista, quit on me. I've been battling a headache, and then my car died.

I just want to go home, get into my comfy clothes, and drink a trough of wine.

Max returns to the SUV and climbs in. "He's good to go. Are you hungry?"

"I'm *so* hungry," Alex says.

"Let me take you out to dinner. Pizza?"

"Pizza! Yes!" Alex says before I can politely decline.

"It's kind of late to cook," Max reminds me, and I nod.

"Pizza would be great."

Max pulls out onto the highway, then turns around to head back into town.

"Are we interrupting your evening?" I ask.

"I was just headed home, and I saw you there, so I decided to rescue you."

I laugh and shake my head. "I had a tow truck on the way."

"And then what?" he asks.

"He would have given us a ride to his shop, and I would have called my mom."

"Well, now you don't have to do that. I'll feed you and give you a ride home."

I settle back against the buttery-soft leather seat and sigh. I won't admit it out loud, but it feels ridiculously good to have someone else take the reins for just a minute.

I close my eyes, listening to Max and Alex talk about school and the little trip I plan to take Alex on for spring break.

I hope I can find more help at the shop by then.

"We're here," Max says, startling me.

"Did I fall asleep?"

"You were snoring and everything," Max replies, making Alex giggle.

"No, you weren't, Mom," Alex says. "Come on, let's eat some pizza."

O'Donnel's Pizza is our favorite place. They've been here for about fifty years, family-owned all that time, and their crust is the best in the world. The restaurant's busy, even for a Tuesday evening, but we get a table right away.

Max and Alex decide on an extra large supreme, and I agree. I *am* hungry.

"Are you okay?" Max asks after he gives Alex five dollars for video games.

"You didn't have to do that," I say.

"The kid's happy and occupied with Pac-Man—which I can't believe they still have—and I can chat with his mom. It's a win-win."

I sigh and nod. Max has a valid point.

"I'm okay. It was a rough day."

"What's up?"

"Besides my car dying on the highway?"

He nods and sips his Coke.

"My employee quit today. Alex's homework is of the devil, and he's only in the third grade, and I've had a headache all day."

"You need food," he says.

"I need a part-time employee," I answer.

"I'm surprised you don't have more help."

"I do during the holidays," I reply. "And in the summer, I'll hire a couple of high school girls. But it's the off-season, and one person has been enough. I'll have my mom come take care of things when I take Alex on vacation."

He just nods, his wheels clearly turning. Max's

business is on a much grander scale than mine. He probably has ten employees who manage his money alone.

"I'm a small business," I remind him.

"I totally get it," he says. "I was just trying to think if I know anyone who might need some part-time work."

"Well, if you do, send them my way."

"Mom! I got the high score!"

"What?" I frown and glance over at the game to see *HIGH SCORE* flashing on the screen. "How is that even possible?"

"I'm brilliant," he says as he sits in the booth next to me. The waitress arrives with our pizza, and we dig in, all of us sighing in happiness after the first bite. "This is so good."

"So good," I agree and move Alex's glass away from his elbow, where I have visions of him spilling it all over the table. "Here's a napkin. Don't wipe your mouth on your sleeve."

"'Kay," he says happily.

It doesn't take us long to fill up on the delicious pizza, then we load up to leave.

"I'll take you home," Max offers.

"Thanks."

He makes sure Alex and I are both buckled in before he pulls off, headed toward my house.

"It's snowed a ton in the hour we were in there,"

I say, surprised that the roads are completely covered.

"They were calling for it," Max says with a nod. "When will you find out about your car?"

"Not until tomorrow afternoon." I blow out a breath. "I'll call my mom and ask her if I can borrow her vehicle."

"No need," Max says. "I have an extra car you can have until this is resolved."

"Absolutely not," I reply, shaking my head.

"So, your mom can be without her vehicle indefinitely?" he asks, and I glare at him, making his lips twitch. "And we have a plethora of car rental places in Cunningham Falls."

"You're a pain in the butt," I say, making him chuckle.

"The car will be at your place in the morning."

I sigh, thinking about everything I have to do tomorrow. Being carless isn't an option.

"I'll pay you for it."

He glances over at me and cocks a brow, then glances back at Alex, who's fallen asleep in the backseat.

"Are you *trying* to piss me off?"

"I would pay for a rental."

"Willa, I'm not using the fucking car," he says quietly. "Just don't kill it, and I'll be happy. I don't want or need your money."

"Thank you," I say as he pulls into my circular driveway. "And thanks for rescuing us. And for the pizza."

"You're welcome."

He hops out when I do and helps me pull a sleepy Alex from the backseat.

"Where is your shovel?" Max asks.

I turn to him to tell him not to worry about it, but he just narrows his eyes at me.

"In the garage. I'll open the door for you."

He nods, and I walk inside, set Alex on his bed, then hurry over to open the garage door. When I return to Alex, he's stripped out of his clothes, but he's sitting on the side of the bed, falling asleep.

"It was a busy day," I say as I tug his pajama top over his head. "Step into the pants, and you can go to sleep."

"I'm not tired," he insists, the way he does every night. But once his pants are pulled on, and he's gone to the bathroom, he hops into bed, and his eyes close immediately.

"Goodnight, Bubba."

"'Night," he says. I shut off his light, but make sure the nightlight comes on before leaving his door open just a crack. I walk out to find that Max has cleared the snow off of my porch and the walkway to the driveway.

"You *are* my hero this evening."

He smiles at me as he leans the shovel against

the wall of the porch.

"Would you like to come in and warm up?" I ask.

His nose is rosy from the cold, and his brown eyes hold mine as he nods his head.

"I'll make you some coffee," I offer.

"I'd better not," he says with a sigh. He reaches out to tuck a piece of my hair behind my ear, sending a shiver down my arms. He smiles softly. "But I'll see you in the morning."

"Okay." I swallow hard, not sure what else to say. I haven't done this in *years.* I'm not even sure what *this* is. Flirting?

Probably.

"What are you thinking so hard about?" he asks.

"I don't even know," I reply honestly. "Thanks again for everything."

"You're welcome." He smiles and turns to jog down the freshly shoveled steps to his sexy SUV. "Sleep well, Wills."

"You, too."

I watch him drive away, then go inside and lean against the closed door.

Oh, my.

CHAPTER FOUR

Willa

"**M**AX IS HERE!" Alex exclaims, holding his Eggo waffle and dripping syrup on his hand while he presses his nose against the glass of the window in the front door. "He's shoveling."

"Get over here and finish your breakfast," I reply, craning my neck to look outside. Sure enough, Max is out there, shoveling away. It snowed about eight inches last night.

"Alex, sit down and eat, then get your socks and shoes on," I say and grab my jacket. "I'm going to say hello to Max."

"I want to say hello."

"After you finish getting ready," I insist, then give him the stern *Mom* look.

"Yes, ma'am," he mumbles, nibbling on his waffle.

"Thank you." I walk onto the front porch and

grin when Max glances over his shoulder at me. "Good morning."

"Yes, it is," he says with a grin. Good God, that expression can still stop me at fifty paces.

"Hi, Noah," I call out to Noah King, who I've also known most of my life. "You guys don't have to shovel."

"I'll bring a snowblower next time," Max says.

"It's not a problem," Noah assures me. "Sorry to hear about your car."

"Thanks. Hopefully, it'll be a quick fix."

Noah nods, then tosses his shovel in the back of his truck after he finishes the last pass down my walkway.

"I'll be right there," Max says to him, then turns to me. "Here is the key fob. You can toss it into your purse and forget about it. You don't need it out to drive the car."

"That's a Range Rover," I inform him with a frown.

"Would you prefer the Mercedes?" he asks. "I can switch them out today if so."

"No. No, that's not it at all." Good God, I'd be even more nervous to drive that car. "This is a Range Rover SUV, Max."

He glances at the vehicle, then back at me with a frown. "Yeah?"

"Never mind," I reply, shaking my head.

"What's wrong?"

"Nothing. Thank you for loaning it to me."

I'm not about to admit to him that driving a car that cost him six figures intimidates the hell out of me. I silently hope and pray that my SUV will be ready quickly.

"Anytime," he says with that charming smile. "Keep it as long as you need it. Do you want me to go over anything with you?"

"I've been driving for a long time," I remind him, making him laugh.

"Yeah, but every vehicle is different. I can show you some things."

"I'll be fine," I insist and see Noah glance at us from inside his truck. "Besides, it looks like Noah needs to get a move on."

"Just call if you need anything," Max says before leaning in to kiss my cheek, setting my body on fire.

Holy Moses, that hasn't happened in a long time.

"Wait!" Alex yells as he runs outside, two different boots on his feet, and no coat on. "I didn't get to say hi yet."

"Well, good morning to you," Max says and ruffles Alex's hair. "Did you sleep well?"

"Oh, yeah," he says with a nod. "I could help shovel."

I smile at my sweet son. He's always been so

ready to jump in and help. He's kind and gracious.

"Noah and I had it covered this time," Max replies with a nod. "But I'll take you up on that next time."

"Cool," Alex says with a smile. "I even have my own shovel."

"It's cold out here," I remind my son, but lean in and kiss his head, breathing in his clean scent. "And we have to get going soon. Did you finish your breakfast?"

"Yeah," he says with a nod. "I'm ready to go."

"We need to fix your boot situation, and you need a coat," I inform him with a laugh. "Thanks again, Max. I'll let you know when I hear from the garage."

"No problem. See you later, Alex."

"Bye!" Alex waves and hurries back inside, slamming the door behind him.

"See you, Wills," Max says with a wink.

"Bye, Max." I wave and follow my son into the house to find that while he did finish his breakfast, he also dumped his backpack on the floor. "What are you doing?"

"I'm just reorganizing things really quick."

"Alex, we don't have time for this. Get everything back into your bag and find your matching boot."

"Which one?"

"Either one." I take a deep breath and remind myself that I'll look back on these moments one day and miss them.

Why are mornings always such a battle?

"You have four minutes," I inform Alex as I tidy up the last of the breakfast mess, pull on my own boots, and fill my favorite travel mug with fresh coffee.

It says *Girl Boss* on the side and was a gift from Jenna, who has a thing for fun mugs.

"Can I have a drink on the way?" Alex asks, watching me put the lid on my mug.

"Sure," I reply. "If you can get yourself together in two minutes."

"I can!" He rushes off, and I pull a disposable cup out of the pantry, brew a cup of hot chocolate in the Keurig, and add some marshmallows to the top before securing the lid. I set it aside to let it cool.

"I do believe we're on time for once," I inform Alex with a smile as we walk out into the snow. I lock the door behind us, and we climb into Max's fancy car.

"Wow, this is super rad," Alex says with a grin. "Max has cool cars."

"Yes, he does," I mutter as I search for the ignition. Max mentioned it's a push-button start, and I find the ignition switch by the steering wheel.

The car roars to life, and I smile back at my

kiddo. "It has vroom."

Alex is playing with his eyetooth.

"What's wrong?"

"It's loose," he says.

Good. That one has been stubborn. "Don't mess with it too much. I don't want it to fall out and have you bleed all over Max's car."

Alex giggles, and I reach over to adjust the mirrors, but the side ones are folded in.

"Hmm, how do I get the mirrors out?" I frown, but can't find the button. It's not in the place it should be. So, I abandon the mirrors and plan to just use the rear-view and be extra cautious.

But then I go to put the car in gear, and there is no gear shift.

None.

Nada.

"Well, crap."

"What's wrong, Mom?"

"I don't know how to put the car in gear," I mutter, getting frustrated. Maybe I should have had Max show me how to drive this damn thing, after all. I had no idea that newer cars were so high-tech. I've ridden in plenty of them, but I've never had to pay attention because I wasn't the driver.

Besides, *my* car is only five years old. It's not ancient.

"You're going to be so late if I can't figure this

out," I mutter as Alex whips his seatbelt off and leans forward, helping me search.

"Here are the letters," he says, pointing to the console to my right. "Push on that circle."

Sure enough, it pops up, and when I turn it to the right, it shifts into Drive.

I just had to have an eight-year-old show me how to drive a car.

Is it too early for wine?

"Thanks, Bubba. Get in your belt."

He grins proudly and buckles up, and we're off. The ride into town is interesting as the car beeps and pulls me away from the lines, trying to drive *for* me.

I'm definitely having my own car fixed. I'm not ready for this technology.

"My seat heats up," Alex says with excitement. I have to admit, it *is* comfortable. And when it's not beeping, it drives smoothly.

I suppose I could learn to drive it if I had to.

I pull up to Alex's school, and he leans over to kiss my cheek before he jumps out of the car and runs toward the teacher at the door. She smiles and waves at me before I pull away and drive the short distance to my shop.

I climb out of the Range Rover and scowl at it as I gather my things and hurry inside. The snow has picked up again, falling in huge flakes the size of quarters.

It's pretty, but it'll be slick to drive in later.

Once inside, I go about my usual routine of flipping on lights and pulling the cash drawer out of the safe and getting it set up. I lay out more coffee pods and make sure the water reservoir is full, then I rearrange a few of the displays to freshen the place up a bit.

Before it's time to open, I check my email to see if anyone has responded to my ad for part-time help and smile when I see three messages from potential employees.

After calling all three and setting up times for interviews, I flip on the *Open* sign and get ready for another day in paradise.

***

"But I only wore it three times." I'm holding a sweater that a customer is trying to return, staring at the burn hole in the hem. "It wasn't my fault that my boyfriend's fire sparked and it landed on me."

But it was my fault?

"Well, I'm glad that you weren't burned," I begin, keeping my temper in check. Alex comes running in the front door. He hurries over to me and drops his book bag behind the counter, then leans in and hugs me.

"Hi, Mom."

"Hi, buddy. Go get your snack and then get started on your homework."

"Okay. I need help with the math." He hurries

away, and I sigh. Today has been another rough one. I've been busy in the shop, which is good, but the customers have been moody and demanding, much like the one standing before me now. And, of course, the garage called to tell me that my car won't be ready for two weeks.

"What are you going to do about this?" the customer asks impatiently.

"Honestly? I'm not going to do anything about it except say I'm sorry that it happened to you. There's no defect in the sweater."

"I only wore it *three times,* and this sweater was more than a hundred dollars."

"It sucks," I agree with a nod.

"I won't shop here again." She glares at me, rips the sweater from my hands, and stomps out of my store.

I breathe a sigh of relief.

"I don't think you'll miss her," Cara King says with a kind smile as she sets a pair of jeans on the counter. Cara is married to Josh King, an older cousin of Noah and Gray King.

The King family is big and has deep roots in Cunningham Falls.

Cara is a teacher in town and a kind woman. She's been a great customer.

"I think you're right."

Once I have the jeans folded and in the bag, I add a pretty pink bow and wish Cara a good day.

"Mom, I need help."

"I know, buddy. Let me just finish with these customers."

Alex sighs and takes a bite of his apple. He's always patient about sharing me with the shop. It was an adjustment for both of us.

The bell above the door dings, and I shrug. "I'm sorry, buddy, it's busy today."

"Hey, Max," Alex says with a smile. "Can you help me with my math?"

"Alex," I admonish and shake my head at Max. "Sorry about that."

"Does he need help with his math?" Max asks.

"Yes," Alex says.

"No," I say at the same time, and Max cocks an eyebrow.

"I do too," Alex insists. "But Mom's too busy with customers."

I shrug a shoulder. "I'll get to it in just a few. Don't worry about it."

"Alex, you go get ready, and I'll be right there," Max says without looking away from me.

"Awesome," Alex says and hurries away to his little desk in my office.

"How are you?" Max asks, watching me closely.

"I'm totally fine," I lie easily and smile at Maisey Henderson, who just walked in with her sister, Brooke.

Max cocks his head to the side, then walks around to stand next to me.

"What's going on?" he asks.

"Just working."

He brushes his knuckles down my cheek, and I swallow hard.

"How has your day been?"

"Great."

He leans in to whisper in my ear. "I will walk through bullshit with you as long as you don't bullshit *me*."

I sigh. "Been a shit day," I whisper back. "And, yes, I could use your help with Alex's homework. It's math."

"I can do math in my sleep," he reminds me, making me grin.

I only passed sophomore trigonometry because of Max.

"I appreciate the help, and I know Alex will get a kick out of it. He likes you."

He smiles. "I like him, too. Almost as much as I like his mama."

And with that, he winks and hurries off to find my son.

"Oh, and your car is possessed!" I yell at Max's back.

He just waves, not looking back at me, and I

can't help but grin.

"Gotta love the Lord for making things like that," Maisey says with a lazy grin as she joins me at the counter, laying a pair of shoes on the glass.

"I don't know what you mean," I reply, doing my best to school my face and ignore the redness in my cheeks.

"Sure, you don't," she says with a snort. "I love these shoes."

"So do I," I reply, happy to change the subject to my favorite topic: fashion. I chat with Maisey and Brooke for about ten minutes before they hurry off.

About thirty minutes before closing time, Max and Alex come out of my office, smiling and joking about something.

It's a bit alarming to see my son enjoying a man who isn't his grandfather. It makes me wonder if I'm doing right by him by not being married.

A boy needs a father.

Before I can think about that in depth, Max says, "Alex and I are going to go get some takeout for dinner so it's ready when you're done here."

"Max, you've done so much already. You really don't have to—"

"Are you going to argue with me every time I try to be helpful?" he asks, leaning on the glass of my counter.

"We're gonna get subs," Alex informs me. I

reach out to smooth the hair on the side of my son's head. It always wants to stand on end. "I want the 'talian one. With pepperoni."

"I suppose subs sound good," I relent and smile at Max. "Thanks. I like turkey."

"Alex told me," he says with a wink. "You let us worry about dinner, and we'll be back in a bit."

"Yeah, let us worry about it, Mom," Alex says before hugging me around the middle and then leading Max to the front door. I stand and watch them leave, pulled from my reverie when my mom's voice surprises me.

"I can handle things here, and you can go with them," she says.

"I didn't know you were here."

"I just came in the back. I wanted to see if you needed my help, but it looks like someone else beat me to the punch."

I sigh and loop my arm through hers. "It's new."

"It's good," she says with a smile. "As long as it's what you want."

"I don't hate it," I admit with a smile.

"Max was always special to you."

"Is the guilt normal?" I ask, knowing that my mom will understand.

"Yes, and you need to let it go, darling girl. Cary would want you to live your life. He wouldn't want you to be alone forever."

"I know," I whisper. "Alex likes Max."

"He is a likeable man. He always was." Mom kisses my cheek. "Want me to close up here?"

"No. There're only thirty minutes left, and it's slowed down. I have interviews tomorrow to fill Krista's position."

"Hire two," she advises me. "You need the help."

I nod, thinking it over. "You're right. Having the extra help would be nice. And it would free me up more in the afternoons with Alex."

"Not to mention if you want to play hooky with a handsome someone whose name rhymes with *fax*."

I giggle, then roll my eyes. "Since when are you such a romantic?"

"Always have been," she says. "And it's time you are, too. Alex is wonderful, but a woman needs more in her life than her children. And you said it yourself, Alex likes him."

"He does. Well, who knows? It might not go anywhere at all."

"Just enjoy him," she advises. "Have a little fun."

She pats my cheek and smiles. "Now, if you don't need me, I'll go get some dinner for Ken and me."

"How is Ken?" I ask. Mom married Ken about five years ago. He's ten years younger than she is and treats her like a queen. It's fun to watch.

"He's wonderful. And most likely hungry."

"Tell him I said hi. Let's get together for dinner this weekend."

"Sounds good to me. I'll make pot roast."

Mom leaves just as Max and Alex come back in. Max hugs my mom in greeting and asks her to give his best to Ken when she sees him.

Yes, Max is a likeable man.

He watches me as he walks my way, his eyes happy and full of humor.

"Mom, we got *four* sandwiches, just in case," Alex says.

"In case of what?" I ask.

"In case we want more," Alex replies with a shrug, just the way Max would, and it makes me laugh.

"It's good to be prepared."

It doesn't take me long to close up shop for the night.

"I'll follow you home," Max says. "It's icy. Be careful."

"Your car—"

"Alex told me all about it," he interrupts, and I stare at my son in surprise.

"You ratted me out?"

Alex giggles, and Max pushes my hair over my

shoulder.

"Do you need a lesson on the car?" he asks.

"Too late. I think I have it figured out now. Oh! Except the mirrors. I can't figure out how to get them to fold out."

His lips twitch as he opens the door and pushes a simple button.

"That was *not* there this morning."

"Buttons do magically appear," he says with a nod, and I bump his hip with mine.

"Don't be a smartass," I mutter, glaring at him in jest.

"Let's go, I'm hungry," Alex says from the backseat of the Range Rover.

"You heard the man," Max says, walking to his Mercedes. "We're hungry."

CHAPTER FIVE

Max

"**W**ILL YOU PLEASE PASS me that paintbrush?" Jenna asks the next day. We're standing in one of her rental properties. The former tenants moved out, and she's sprucing it up for the next ones.

I hand her the brush, and she gets to work painting the trim on the window in the master bedroom.

"How much do you rent this for?" I ask, looking around. The house is older, in an original neighborhood in Cunningham Falls. It's near schools and downtown.

"Fifteen hundred," she replies with a smile. "I snatched it up when the market was down."

"You could get more than that."

"Not everyone can afford more than that," she reminds me with a shrug. "It covers the mortgage and the upkeep with a little extra, so it's fine. If you want to start on that wall, the roller is over there."

"How did I get roped into this?"

She offers me a bright smile.

"You love me, *and* you miss me. This way, you get to spend time with me."

"You're engaged to a movie star, and your brother has more money than any one person should. We could pay someone to do this."

She stares out the window for a second, contemplating, then shrugs again. "I like to do it. You don't have to paint if you don't want to. Just chat with me."

"I can do both," I reply, loading the paint on the roller, then gliding it onto the wall.

"How's Willa?" she asks.

"Beautiful," I reply immediately. "Funny. Sexy. Smart."

"But how do you really feel?" she asks with a laugh. "I think it's great you're spending time together again. Do you like Alex?"

"He's great." I turn back to the tray of paint to reload my roller. "She's done a good job of raising him. He's not a brat, he has manners, and he's a kick in the butt."

"Alex is the best," Jenna agrees. "He's so fun-loving and sweet."

"Like his mom," I say softly. "But I see a lot of Cary in him, as well."

"Agreed," Jenna says with a sigh before taking a sip of her coffee and examining her handiwork. "They're a cute little package."

"And I'm squarely in the friend zone," I say in disgust. "I don't think I can do it, Jen."

"Be her friend?"

"Be *just* her friend. She's still the most amazing person I've ever known. I don't want to be her buddy."

"Of course, you don't," Jenna says, surprising me. "Willa was never just your friend, Max. She was your girl. It makes absolute sense that you want more now."

"I don't know what to do about it," I admit. "She fights me at every turn. I offer to help with things, simple things, and she immediately puts up a wall and says, 'that's okay.' She's so damn stubborn."

"It's been just her for nine years," Jenna reminds me. "She's had to depend on herself. Yes, she has parents and friends who help, but it's not the same as having a partner. So, it makes sense that she is resistant to accept help from a man. A man that she has feelings for but who hasn't been a part of her life in a very long time."

"Are you a shrink now?" I ask, setting the roller down and propping my hands on my hips.

"I'm smart," she says. "You're not the only one in the family with brains. So, here's the million-dollar question."

"I'll pay you a million dollars if we can change the subject," I reply, making her snort.

"Why haven't you asked her out?"

I blink at her, then scowl. "Because this is *Willa.*"

"And?"

"And up until a couple weeks ago, we weren't even speaking."

"You are now." She sips her coffee. "And Willa is a woman, Max. Not just a mom or your old girlfriend. She's a woman who wants some romance. Even if she doesn't know it yet."

"Huh." I rub my hand over the back of my neck. "Why didn't I think of that?"

"Because you're smart, but you're too stuck in your head. You romanced her once before, and it worked because she was head over heels in love with you. Do what you did then but on steroids. Court her."

"That's not a bad idea." I check the time on my Apple watch and grin. "It's lunchtime."

"Are you thinking of food *now*?" she asks.

"No. I'm going to take Willa some lunch and ask her out."

"Atta boy," she says, offering me her fist to bump. "Go get your girl."

"Are you sure you don't want me to stay and paint?"

"Yeah, I do want you to stay and paint," she replies, making me pause and stare at her. "Kidding. Get out of here. I'll call Willa later and get all the details."

I grin, then hurry out of the house and to my SUV. If I remember correctly, Willa could never resist the tacos from José's, so I swing through there and order her favorite—chicken tacos with chips and salsa—then walk down the block to Willa's shop.

The bell over the door dings as I walk inside. There are no customers, and Willa isn't behind the counter. I set the bag down and go looking for her.

"That won't work for me," I hear her say. She's in her office and on the phone. She sees me walk in and smiles, holding her finger up to signal that she'll be just a minute. "I ordered those blouses ten days ago and paid for overnight shipping. You'll refund all of my money *and* send the blouses, today, or I pull my business from you altogether. And that's a lot of lost money for you. …That's right. See that you do."

She hangs up, crosses something off her to-do list, and smiles at me.

"Hi," she says.

"That was damn sexy," I reply. I want to pull her against me and kiss the ever-loving hell out of her, but this isn't the time or place for that.

Not yet.

But soon.

"Me complaining is sexy?"

"You running your business like a damn boss is sexy." I drag my knuckles down her cheek. "I'm proud of you, Wills."

Her cheeks redden, and she offers me a shy smile.

"I don't like people who don't run their business well," she admits. "And this distributor has been on my last nerve."

"Time to find a new one." I take her hand and lead her out of her office. "I hope you're hungry because I brought food."

"You feed me a lot," she says, but her eyes light up when she sees the bag from José's. "Chicken tacos?"

"Of course."

"You know I can't resist these."

I laugh as she tears into the bag and takes a bite of her taco. "I know."

I clear my throat, suddenly as nervous as I was the first time I asked her out when I was sixteen.

"I also came by to ask you out," I blurt. Willa stops chewing and stares at me with wide, brown eyes. "Why do you look like a deer caught in the headlights?"

She shakes her head and swallows the bite in her mouth.

"Like, on a date?"

I smile, trying to hide the fact that her lack of enthusiasm is killing my ego.

"That's usually how it works, yes."

She scoops some salsa onto a chip but just stares at it while she seems to think it over.

"If you'd rather not—"

"That would be fun," she says at the same time.

"Friday night?"

She nods. "Sure. What time?"

"Six," I reply, an idea taking shape in my head.

"I'll be ready," she says with a sweet smile. "And thanks for lunch."

"You're welcome."

***

Her porch lights are on, and my Range Rover is parked in front of the garage. It's snowed every day, so I stopped by while she was at work to shovel for her.

I don't like the idea of her working her ass off all day, then coming home and doing more. I know she has enough to do with Alex.

Shoveling is the least I can do.

Willa's home is a beautiful farmhouse that sits on about ten acres. When you think of the houses on Christmas cards, well, this is what you see.

It's tasteful and pretty, just like Willa.

I get out of my car, smooth my hands down my

jacket, and take a deep breath.

You'd think I'd never been on a date before.

I just don't want to fuck this up. This is *Willa.*

I climb the steps to the porch and ring the doorbell. When Willa answers the door, I just about swallow my tongue.

She's in a pretty pink sweater that falls off one shoulder, black leggings, and grey boots that go up to her knees.

"Hey," she says with a smile, stepping back to let me inside. "I'm just about ready. Mom just left with Alex."

"Sleepover?" I ask, my dick twitching at the thought of Willa being free all night long.

Calm the fuck down, Hull.

"Yes, and he was excited. He was also sure to remind me to ask you to come to his birthday party tomorrow afternoon. No obligation, of course."

"I'd love to," I reply honestly, relieved that I thought to pick him up a present earlier this week. "What time should I be here?"

"It starts at two. There will be a herd of young boys here, my mom and Ken, and Cary's parents on FaceTime."

"That's cool," I reply. "I'll be here at two."

She grins and drapes her jacket over her arm, then reaches for her small purse and nods. "I'm set."

"Perfect."

I wait while she locks her house, then open the car door for her. Once she's settled in her seat, I shut the door and hurry around to the driver's side.

"What's on tap for tonight?" she asks as I pull away from her house.

"I thought we'd start with dinner at Ed's." I glance over to see her lips tip up in a grin. "And maybe a movie after."

"So, our first date all over again?"

"Is that too cheesy?"

She laughs. "Not at all. It's actually really sweet. And comfortable."

I reach over and link her fingers with mine, the same way I did on that first date, and she sighs happily, gripping my fingers in return.

"You do have a nicer car now," she admits.

"You didn't like my old Datsun truck?"

"I mean, it was fine. It got us around. But it didn't have heated seats or satellite radio."

"It didn't have a radio at all," I reply with a laugh. "And it broke down more than it ran."

"I think that's how first cars are supposed to be," she says with a shrug. "Maybe I'll feel differently when it's time for Alex to have a vehicle. Thank God we're a few years out from that."

I blink, thinking about Alex as a teenager. I hope I'm still a part of their lives then. I'd happily buy him any car he wants.

"Speaking of cars, have you heard anything on yours?"

"Still at least a week until it's finished," she says with a sigh. "If you need the Rover back, I'm sure I can borrow my mom's."

"That's not why I was asking. You can keep it."

She stares at me in shock. "Until my car is done."

"Sure."

I glance over to find her eyes narrowed.

"You didn't mean I can keep it forever."

"What if I did?"

"I'd laugh and ask you if you've been drinking."

My lips twitch. Most of the women I've dated over the past ten years would have simply said, *"thanks, I'll keep it."*

Not Willa.

"I don't need it."

"Then why did you buy it?" she asks.

"Good question." I sigh and slow down to stop at a red light. "Because I can? Does that make me sound like an asshole?"

"No, it makes you sound rich," she replies.

"I am rich, Wills. No more Datsun trucks for me. I can buy pretty much anything in the world."

"I have so many questions," she says with a smile. "And not in a bad way, in a truly curious way."

"Let's get inside, and you can ask me anything you like," I say as I park outside Ed's Diner and escort her in. We're given the booth in the back corner, the same one we always sat at when we were kids.

"Did you do this on purpose?" Willa asks.

"Nope, just coincidence," I reply.

Of course, I did it on purpose.

But a man has to have a few secrets and tricks up his sleeve.

"Can I get y'all something to drink?" the waitress asks.

"Chocolate shake for me," I say.

"Can I share yours?" Willa asks, making me grin.

"One chocolate shake it is," I say. The waitress nods and leaves us with our menus. "What are those questions of yours?"

"Let me start by saying, I'm so proud of you, Max."

I stare at her, surprised. This isn't what I expected at all.

"You grew up middle-class like the rest of us. And you took advantage of every opportunity to get an excellent education, to work your butt off, and it's paid off for you in spades. I'm not just talking about the money, but all of your success. You're respected, and you've earned all of that and more."

"Geez, Wills. You're embarrassing me."

"And now for the good stuff," she says, leaning in after the waitress drops off our shake. It's huge, and there's more in the steel malt cup she brought with it. "What's it like to have that much money? I mean, I do pretty well, but I still have a budget, and I have a small retirement plan and a college fund for Alex, that sort of thing. What you have is on a whole other level."

I nod, trying to think of how to explain it.

"Honestly, it's like everything is free for me."

Her eyebrows climb into her bangs.

"Really."

"Really," I confirm. "When I spend money, it doesn't matter. I don't even have to think about it because no matter how much I spend, it'll never make a dent in my bottom line. Does that make sense?"

"Yeah," she says with a nod. "It does."

"But, I also enjoy the game of the financials, so I have a team of accountants who help me with investments and taxes."

"I don't even want to *think* about your taxes," she says, shaking her head.

"No. You don't." I laugh and reach out to take her hand in mine again, needing the skin-on-skin contact. "I love to invest, so I have real estate all over the world."

"Where?" she asks.

"Here, California, Seattle, New York, London, and Paris. I've been looking at a cabin on Lake Tahoe."

"Wow," she breathes. "That is a lot."

"But at the end of the day, I'm still just me," I insist as our burgers and fries are set in front of us. "I love French fries with ketchup and my coffee black."

"Ew."

"No ketchup?"

"No black coffee. I need it sweet."

I grin. "I like to go on dates with my beautiful Willa, and I love my little town."

"So, you're just Max with a lot of money."

"Yep."

"That's not why I'm here." Her face is serious now. "I don't care about the money, Max. I'm proud of you, and happy for you, but that's not—"

"I know," I say, squeezing her hand, then letting go so we can eat. "That's one of the reasons why we're here tonight."

"How are your parents?" she asks. "I didn't get to talk to them much at Brad's wedding."

"You probably know that they live most of the year down in Arizona now," I begin. Willa nods, and we spend the next half hour enjoying our food and talking about our families. Our businesses.

Alex.

"He's started drawing pictures of puppies and sticking them on the fridge. He thinks he's being nonchalant," Willa says with a laugh. "Like I don't notice the new pictures every couple of days."

"He's campaigning for what he wants," I say with a smile. "He's smart. Is it working?"

"It's all in vain," she says with a laugh. "I chose a puppy weeks ago. We're going to go pick it up tomorrow after his party."

"He'll be over the moon," I say. "You're an excellent mom, Willa."

Her eyes suddenly fill with tears.

"Shit, what did I say?"

"Nothing bad," she says, dabbing at her eyes. "Thank you. Being a mom is hard. Harder than I ever thought it would be, and there are days that I don't think I'm very good at it."

"Have you seen Alex?" I ask. "He's great. A lot of that is because you've done your job."

"I'm lucky," she says, her eyes drying up. Thank God. I never could stand to see her cry. "Alex was an easy baby. So laid-back and sweet. He wasn't colicky or high-maintenance. It was like the universe knew that I was already a wreck, and it cut me some slack."

"I'm glad," I murmur. "Should we get out of here?"

"Sure." She stands, reaches for her purse, and I follow her out to my car.

"Can I take you somewhere else?" I ask.

"Of course. Where do you want to go?"

"Paris."

I watch as she goes pale, and her mouth drops, making me laugh.

"Just kidding. We'll save that for another time. I'd like to take you to the movies."

She laughs and reaches over to smack my shoulder.

"Ouch. I don't remember you being this violent."

"I don't even have a passport."

"Oh, sweetheart, we need to change that."

She doesn't say anything as we pull away from the diner and head toward my house. I know this is a lot, and moving fast, but I don't know any other way to be with Willa.

I stayed away for so long, it's like I feel as if I have to make up for lost time.

I pull into my garage and cut the engine.

"Uh, I thought we were going to the movies?"

"We are." I grin and hop out of the vehicle, then open the door for her and lead her inside. "You've been here before with Jenna."

"True, I have," she says with a nod. "You've never been here."

"Well, now I can give you a proper tour."

It takes us a half hour to make our way through the big house on the lake. The last room is the theater room with a popcorn machine, candy, and soda. It's decorated with movie posters, including one of the show we're going to see tonight.

I did that on purpose, too.

"Do you want popcorn?"

"Of course," she says. "And Milk Duds."

Just like that first date.

"Coming right up." I toss her the Duds, put in some fresh popcorn to pop, and cue the Blu-ray disk.

"What are we watching?" she asks.

"You don't remember what we saw on our first date?"

She frowns. "It's been about fifteen years, Max. I don't remember."

"*Pirates of the Caribbean*," I reply as I pass her some popcorn and a soda. I hit play on the remote, and the lights go down, the curtain goes up, and the screen comes to life.

"Leave it to you to have a real movie theater in your house," she says playfully.

"It's handy," I say. "Besides, we could have watched this in my car on my iPad. We went to the drive-in on that first date."

"It's a bit cold for that," she concedes and

snuggles up against me on the soft red loveseat in the middle of the room. "And this way, we can snuggle."

Or, I could lay her back, strip her bare, and fuck her right here in my theater.

Instead, I shove some popcorn into my mouth and watch as Captain Jack Sparrow slurs his way through the movie.

After Willa sets her empty popcorn bucket aside, I yawn, stretch my arm high over my head, then drop it over her shoulders.

She gives me the side-eye, but her lips are tipped up in a grin.

My fingers play against the soft skin of her bare shoulder before moving up into her silky hair. Her chest rises and falls in a deep sigh, and I know she's as turned on as I am.

Using my moves from back in the day, I lean in and press a kiss to her earlobe. The next thing I know, she's turned, plunged her hand in my hair, and my lips are on hers, hard and sure, drinking her in like I've been lost in the desert for a month.

She's sweet, giving, and so damn *good*. She hasn't changed at all.

I need her. All of her.

When we come up for air, her forehead is pressed to mine, and we're both breathing hard.

"God, I've missed you," I whisper.

"Me, too," she whispers back.

CHAPTER SIX

Willa

"TELL ME EVERYTHING,"** Jenna hisses next to me. We're at yoga the morning after my date with her brother, in the back where we always are during class.

"Take a deep breath, everyone," Fallon McCarthy, our yoga instructor, says from the front of the classroom. There are maybe ten of us here today, including Brooke and Maisey Henderson, Jillian King, and Lauren Sullivan. "And exhale. Beautiful. Reach way up…"

"It was a first date," I whisper loudly. "Literally. He recreated our first date from back in the day."

"Oh my God, that's sweet," Brooke says. "Sorry. I'm totally eavesdropping."

"We all are," Jillian replies with a laugh. "Max and I have been friends for years."

Fallon glances back at us, but just when I think she's going to yell at us for chatting during class, she just smiles.

"I don't care if we chat about Willa's love life, as long as we do it while we yoga," she says, making us laugh. "Let's do some cat and cow poses, ladies. Let's strengthen those cores and backs."

"So, tell us about the first date," Lauren says.

"We had dinner at Ed's. We shared a chocolate shake and each ordered burgers and fries. Just like before."

"Damn, I'm trying to shed some of this baby weight, and she's talking about burgers and fries from Ed's," Lauren mumbles.

"And then we went to his house to watch *Pirates of the Caribbean*. We watched it at the drive-in back then, but it's a bit cold for that now."

"Does he really have his own movie theater?" Maisey asks.

"Yeah. It's gorgeous," Jenna replies. "We'll have a girls' night over there sometime and watch a bunch of chick flicks."

"I'm in," Maisey says with a smile.

"Downward dog," Fallon instructs us.

"I bet Max knows all about downward dog," Brooke says, making me choke on my own spit. I fall to my knees and cough, trying to catch my breath.

"That's disgusting," Jenna says. "He's my

brother, Brooke."

"He's not *our* brother," Jillian says with a laugh. "And Willa would know all about his downward dog abilities."

"Can't breathe," I stutter, laughing and coughing at the same time.

"Gross. Ew. Tell them you've never seen my brother naked," Jenna demands, but all I can do is shake my head as I take a deep breath.

"It's been a long time, but yes, I've seen him naked."

"Just think about how much better it'll be now," Lauren says thoughtfully.

Oh, trust me, I have.

His body is so different. He grew a couple of additional inches after he graduated from high school, and man, has he filled out! The muscles are ridiculous. I couldn't help but try to touch him everywhere last night when he was kissing the life out of me.

And that groping was over the clothes. I can't even imagine how good he'll look and feel naked.

"Oh, no, she's thinking about it." Jenna snaps her fingers in front of my face. "Earth to Willa. Wake up."

"Sorry. It's hard not to think about it. But, no sex with him yet."

"Or ever," Jenna says, scowling.

"On your backs," Fallon says, "and into the

happy baby pose."

We grab our feet and let our legs fall wide.

"Now, I can't stop thinking about sex and yoga poses," Maisey says. "Is it just me, or is this very sexual?"

"Yoga helps with sex," Fallon offers with a smile. "Being more flexible and open to feelings makes intimacy incredible."

"I'm coming to yoga every day," Brooke says, making us giggle.

"Fallon, you're the best," I say as I stretch my legs out and lay flat on my back. "Most instructors would yell at us for being immature during class."

"You're all fun," she replies happily. "This is a space for acceptance and rejuvenation. If you reach that by being a little silly with your friends, who am I to say that's wrong? Take a deep breath, now, and sit up into meditation pose, legs crossed."

We breathe some more, and are finally quiet for a few moments.

"That's class for today," Fallon says cheerfully. "Have a wonderful Saturday. *Namaste*, friends."

"*Namaste*."

"Good luck, Willa," Jillian says with a smile. "Not that you need it. Max has been gone over you for years."

"He looks at you like you're a new computer," Lauren agrees. "And that's pretty great, because he loves his computers."

Jenna and I laugh, waving goodbye to the others, and gather our things to head out.

"What's on tap now?" she asks me.

"I have to go pick up Alex from my mom's, then take him home and get ready for his party. He invited eight little boys to come over, and they're going to build snow forts."

"Fun," she says with a smile. "Your property is perfect for it."

"It really is. I'll have a hot chocolate bar set up for them because that's one of Alex's favorite things, and cake, of course."

"Max is excited to come," she says with a wink.

"He'll have a rude awakening when he has to watch me wrangle nine little boys." I shrug. "I guess he has to see the not-so-sexy sides of my life too, huh?"

"I don't think he'll find you being a good mom unattractive," Jenna replies. "I know that he admires you very much for being a good mother."

"He said that last night," I agree with a sigh. "And then I was stupid and cried over it because it surprised me."

"I'm sure he didn't think it was stupid."

"He looked mildly terrified," I admit and shrug. "He never knew what to do with me when I cried."

"No, Max isn't good with tears. So, he's coming to the party today, but do you know when you'll get to have more one-on-one time with him?"

"No," I say, shaking my head. "That's the tough thing, Jenna. I have a kiddo, and I *like* spending time with him. I'm not willing to farm him out to my mom all the time because I want to go on dates."

"I don't think it needs to be that extreme," she says with a frown. "Max likes Alex. But maybe you could *farm him out* a couple of evenings a month so you can have an adult dinner with a handsome guy."

"True. Last night was fun, and if I'm honest, I needed it. Not having to worry about someone spilling their soda or wiping their mouth was a nice break."

"Max rarely spills his soda," Jenna agrees. "And if he ever has an issue with spending time with both you and Alex, well, he's not the guy for you."

"You're right." I nod, feeling better. "You're absolutely right. So, time will tell. Because Alex is wonderful in small doses, but when real life hits? Fevers and exhaustion, and not getting his way? They're not often, but they do happen, and it's not fun."

"Like you said, time will tell," she says. "I'm just happy to see you dropping your walls with him."

"I'm not doing that," I insist. "I *can't* do that, Jenna. The walls are there for a reason. If he wants to get inside of them, he has to make the effort, and I will admit that he's doing a good job of making an effort. I've done my share of resisting."

"Are you going to keep resisting?"

"It's hard not to. It's just been me for so long."

"I know. I reminded him of that, too. Just remember, if Max offers to help you in any way, it's because he wants to. He doesn't do much that he doesn't want to do."

"I'm slowly remembering that." I take a deep breath and pull Jenna in for a hug. "Thank you, for being an amazing best friend, despite the fact that I make drama with your brother."

"Oh, honey, this isn't drama. Have you seen *The Bachelor*? That's drama. I love you. Tell Alex I'll bring him his present in a couple of days."

"Will do. See you later."

***

"We made the *best* fort!" Alex exclaims as he runs into the house, followed by three of his friends. Their cheeks are rosy, and their eyes are shining in excitement.

All of the kids will sleep well tonight.

"We made *six* forts," Pierce, Alex's best friend, reminds him. "And we have to build a road that connects them."

"Can I get my sled out so we can drag it over the snow and pack it down?" Alex asks. "That'll be the road."

"You can do that after cake and presents," I reply with a smile, tugging his stocking cap off and smoothing down his hair. "Go let your guys know to come in for a while. And shed all of the gear in the garage. I'd rather not have a wet mess in the house."

"Yes, ma'am," Alex says excitedly. "C'mon, guys!"

They hurry back outside.

"We have about ten minutes to finish this up," I inform Max, who's standing next to me, watching the boys outside with longing in his eyes. "You can go play with them if you want."

I bump his hip with mine as I move to uncover the cake and put the candles in it.

"I'm happy in here, helping you."

My cell phone rings.

"That'll be Jean and Dan. They always Face-Time in so they can watch Alex with his cake and presents."

"That's awesome," Max says with a grin. "I haven't talked to them in a while. I'll take the phone, and you finish this."

"Thanks." I offer Max a grateful smile as he accepts the call.

"Hi, Ms. Monroe," Max says to Jean. "I am answering so Willa can finish getting the cake ready."

"It's wonderful to see you, Max. How are you?"

"I can't complain at all." Max walks out of the kitchen, his voice fading with him.

"I've always liked Max," my mom murmurs next to me as she unwraps paper plates and cups with dinosaurs on them.

I just smile at her.

"He's handsome, too." She winks at me.

"I'm not having this conversation in the middle of my child's birthday party," I whisper, making her laugh. "Is the hot chocolate gone?"

"Oh, yeah, they blew through that in the first thirty minutes," she says.

"Perfect. They can have juice with their cake."

We set about pouring juice into the cups and setting the dining room table—currently covered in a vinyl *Star Wars* tablecloth—with the plates, silverware, and drinks. There's a sack full of party favors for each guest, and in addition to the cake decorated by Maisey, I have cupcakes, just in case we need extra.

I learned early to always be prepared going into a child's birthday party.

Alex's place is at the head of the table, so I set the cake there so he can blow out the candles.

"It's going to be so cool," a little boy named Zane says as the boys start to pour into the house. They shed their winter gear in the garage like I asked and come running to the dining room.

"You can sit anywhere you want," I inform them. "Are you ready for some cake?"

"Yeah!" they exclaim.

Goodness, nine-year-old boys can make a lot of noise. My ears may never stop ringing.

"Alex, you're up here, buddy." My kiddo joins me, sitting in his chair, and I light his candles. "Say hi to Nana and Papa." I gesture to Max, who's pointing my phone at us.

"Hi," Alex says, smiling and waving. "I'm going to blow out the candles now."

"Okay, boys, let's sing."

The birthday song may not be perfectly harmonized or even in the right key, but it's heartfelt and makes my boy feel like a million bucks. And when the song is over, he scrunches his eyes closed tightly to make his wish and then blows all nine candles out on the first try.

Max passes my phone to Alex so he can talk to Nana and Papa while I cut the cake, and my mom passes it out to the boys, who all dig in like rabid dogs.

There's not even one drop of juice spilled—a miracle in and of itself—and within fifteen minutes, every crumb of cake has been devoured, green and orange icing is on every kiddo's face, and the plates have been cleared away.

"Present time!" my mom announces. She walks over to us, holding her phone up to take photos. Ken and Max are still on the other side of the room, talking with Jean and Dan.

This might be the best birthday party I've ever thrown for Alex.

I purposefully save my present for last. When all of the other gifts have been opened, I drag a huge box out of my bedroom, wrapped in *Star Wars* wrapping paper.

"Holy cow, Mom," Alex says, his eyes wide. "It's huge!"

"Do you need help opening it?"

"Heck, no," he says. My eyes find Max's, and we share a smile. Alex tears into the paper, opens the box, and frowns. "A dog bed?"

"What else?"

I peer into the box with him as he pulls out more dog supplies.

"A leash. Some dog toys and treats."

"I wonder if this present came to the wrong house?" I ask, frowning in mock confusion.

"Mom." Alex takes my cheeks in his little hands and looks me dead in the eyes. "Don't play with my emotions."

"I wouldn't do that."

"Does this mean I get a dog?"

I can tell he's holding his breath, waiting for me to answer.

"We go pick him up later today," I confirm. Suddenly, my nine-year-old has launched into my arms, holding on tightly. He doesn't even care that all of his friends are watching.

"Thank you, thank you, thank you," he says,

squirming while hugging me fiercely. "This is the best birthday *ever.*"

"You're welcome." I kiss his cheek. "I love you, Bubba."

"I love you too, Mom. Guys! I get a puppy! What should I name him?"

The boys start throwing out names like Rocky and George, and I start to clear the mess off the table.

"You guys have one more hour to finish your forts," I inform them, and they scramble back to the garage to put on their gear and get back out to play.

"Well, that went perfectly," Jean says when I get on the phone with her. "He's so excited."

"I am, too, honestly," I reply. "I always had a dog growing up. It'll be good for him."

"Thanks for letting us join you," Dan says and blows me a kiss. "Enjoy the rest of your day."

"And send us photos later of our boy with the puppy," Jean adds.

"I definitely will," I promise.

***

"Where is the puppy?" Alex asks from the backseat of the Range Rover, bouncing in his seat.

"It's not too far away."

Max is driving, and I'm in the passenger seat as if we're just a normal family going to pick up their new puppy.

It's an odd sensation, and one that I like a little too much.

"We'll be there in about six minutes," Max says.

"What kind of a puppy is it?" Alex asks, making me laugh.

"Hang in there for six minutes, and you'll see for yourself," I reply.

"I can't stand it," Alex says. "I'm just too excited."

"I know. But we need to talk. Remember what I said before."

"Mom, I totally understand. I have to be responsible and take care of him and love him always."

"Why am I potty training in the winter?" I ask Max, suddenly horrified. "And why didn't I think of this before?"

"Because your son's birthday is in the winter," he says with a shrug. "It won't be so bad."

"You won't be the one outside with it at five in the morning with a wind chill of negative forty."

I sigh and drag my hand down my face.

"I'll do it, Mom."

No, you won't. Because I won't allow it.

Max pulls into a driveway, and when we reach the house, he cuts the engine.

"You wait here," I insist. "I just want to make

sure they're ready for us."

I hop out and knock on the door. I can hear barking inside, some from adult dogs, and some from the babies, and it makes me grin.

"Willa," Sandy Gustafson, my former eighth-grade history teacher says as she opens her door. "I have the little guy ready for you."

"Do you mind if Alex comes in to meet him?" I ask.

Sandy smiles. "Not at all."

I wave for both of the guys to join me. Alex runs up the steps as if he's escaping the zombie apocalypse, coming to an abrupt halt at my side.

"Alex, this is Mrs. Gustafson."

"Hi," he says shyly.

"Hello there," Sandy says, holding her hand out for his. "Would you like to come and see the cutest puppies ever?"

"Yes, please."

I smile up at Max as we follow Sandy and Alex inside to the back of the house, where she has an entire family room gated off for the dogs. She has five pups now, and the mama in the room with them.

"Oh, wow!" Alex breathes. "Which one is mine?"

"The one with the blue bow tied on his collar," Sandy says, pointing to the little fella who's play-ing with his sibling, biting on her ear.

Being Basset Hounds, their ears are long and droopy, their legs short. They are also incredibly adorable.

"Oh, I love him," Alex whispers. "Can I go in?"

"You bet." Sandy opens the gate, and Alex carefully walks inside, approaches his pup, and sits on his butt, laughing when puppies immediately crawl all over him, snuggling and playing.

"Mom!" Alex laughs again and kisses the cheek of a puppy. "They like me."

"Best birthday ever," Max says with a grin. He wraps his arm around my shoulders. "You did good, Mom."

"Yeah." I wipe a tear of joy from my cheek. "Who cares about early morning potty training in the snow?"

CHAPTER SEVEN

Willa

I'LL TAKE HIM OUT," Max offers. We've had the puppy for almost a full week, and it's more work than I ever anticipated.

I feel like I have a newborn *and* a toddler.

"Thanks." I smile in gratitude and return to browning the meat on the stove. Alex is at Pierce's house for the night, having a sleepover. Which means, I have the puppy *and* Max for the night.

I'm nervous as a virgin on her first date. The chemistry between Max and me is as strong as it ever was. Maybe even stronger.

And with no kid at home tonight, there *will* be nudity.

Please, God, let there be nakedness.

But first, there's dinner and puppy detail.

My phone rings, and I frown at the number. It's

the mechanic.

"Hello."

"Hey, Willa, it's Tom. Say, I know I promised you the car back by Wednesday, but it looks like it's going to take longer."

I sigh and rub my hand over my face.

"How much longer?"

"At least another week. I'm sorry to do that to you; we're still waiting on parts."

"How is it taking this long?"

"We live in the boonies, Willa," he says, laughing in my ear. "Everything takes a long time. But I'll let you know when the parts get here."

"Thanks. Keep me posted."

I hang up and sigh just as Max comes back in with Rocky, the name Alex settled on for his pup.

"What's up?" Max asks as Rocky runs over to his water dish.

"That's it, drink more water and pee on my rug again," I mutter, shaking my head. "Why don't they make diapers for puppies?"

"Good question," Max says, wrapping his arms around me from behind and burying his face in my neck, sending shivers over every damn inch of my body. "What's wrong?"

"Tom called. No car by Wednesday."

"Did he say why?"

"Still waiting on parts. I don't get it, Max. My

car isn't that old."

"Maybe they sent him the wrong ones to start with," he suggests, his hands gliding down my sides to my hips. I suddenly don't care about my car anymore. "This smells great."

"Tacos always were your favorite."

"Yeah, the tacos smell good, too." He grins against my skin, and I want to turn in his arms and strip him naked, then have my way with him.

But the ground beef is sizzling, so I turn my attention to dinner, sprinkling taco seasoning and water over the meat and giving it a stir.

"The puppy is quiet," I announce, looking around in panic.

"I'm on it," he says, leaving me to see where the little terrorist ran off to. "Found him."

"What's he doing?"

"You don't want to know."

I blow out a breath while I question my life choices.

"You'll need to replace the rug after he grows out of this puppy phase."

"Did he pee on it again? You just took him out."

"No, he chewed the corner."

"Damn it." I glare at the little thing and shake my spatula at him. "It's a good thing you're so cute."

"Arf," Rocky replies, panting happily and

snuggling against Max's chin.

"In the crate for him while we eat. He can have a chew bone and his rope toy."

Max gets Rocky settled, and I dish up dinner.

"I guess I didn't realize how much Alex does for Rocky," I admit. "He's really done a good job of taking care of that dog."

"What do you do with him during the day when Alex is at school, and you're at work?"

I cringe. "I've been taking him to the shop. I said I wouldn't do that, but he's just a baby. He shouldn't be in that crate, alone, all day long. So, I have a bed, leash, and crate for him at work."

"You're a sucker," Max says with a laugh.

"Would *you* leave him home alone for sometimes ten hours at a time?"

He seems to think it over, chewing his tacos. "No. That's a long time."

"Exactly. My hope is that as he gets older and calms down a bit, he'll be easier."

"It will be," Max assures me.

He clears the dishes when we're finished eating. I check on Rocky, who has his nose pressed to the edge of the crate as if to say, "*help me! I'm in prison.*"

I let him out, scoop him up, and we go into the living room to turn on the TV.

"Want to watch a movie?" I ask Max when he

walks in from the kitchen, carrying two mugs of coffee. "Mm, thanks."

"We can watch whatever you like," he says as he sits next to me. The way the man fills out a pair of jeans should be illegal. And when you add that black Henley with the sleeves pushed up on his forearms, well...

Hello, sex on a stick.

Rocky abandons me for Max, turns a circle, and falls asleep in his lap.

Little traitor.

I flip through the movie channels as we sip our coffee.

"I like your house," Max says.

"Thank you."

"It's not at all like I remember it."

I nod and set the remote aside, mid-search. Looks like it'll be *Armageddon* in the background.

I reach over and mute Bruce Willis and then turn to Max.

"I've done a lot of work to it. When Cary and I bought it, we knew it was a fixer-upper. But we loved the property, and the size of the house was great."

"Agreed. How much square footage do you have?"

"Almost four thousand," I reply with a smile. "And one of the perks of being on my own large property outside of town? I can add on or do pretty much anything I want. The permits from the county aren't as strict as in the city limits."

"I learned that last year," Max says, shaking his head. "I wanted to add a boathouse, and the city threw a fit."

"Don't you have a boathouse?"

"No, I have a covered lift, which is okay. But I'd like to store the boats out of the elements on my property in the winter. A boathouse is the most efficient way to do that."

I nod as if I understand. There are moments when I'm reminded just how wealthy Max is.

"But we're not talking about my boathouse." He reaches out and twists a strand of my hair around his finger. "Tell me more about your house."

"Well." I clear my throat. "It's finally just the way I want it. The new kitchen and master bathroom went in last year. I tore down the walls that separated the kitchen and main living area because I wanted an open concept. The beam that I had to put in was not cheap, but so worth it."

"It's beautiful," he agrees, looking around the space. "I like the farmhouse feel."

"Well, it's no mansion on the lake, but we like it."

"Don't do that," Max says softly. "What you've built here is impressive and beautiful. It has your heart in it. That's more than I can say about my house at the lake."

"You're right," I reply with a nod. "I am proud of my home. And I'm glad you like it."

His eyes are pinned to mine as he leans in and brushes his lips over my own, back and forth, then he sinks in, kissing me lazily. His lips are soft, taking my mouth on the dance of a lifetime.

Max always did know how to kiss the pants off me.

Suddenly, there's an extra slurp, right on our lips.

"Hey, buddy, you're messing with my mojo here," Max says, petting Rocky on the head. Rocky doggy-grins and boosts himself up to kiss my chin.

"Yes, you like to kiss." I plant one on the puppy's cheek. "Don't you?"

"I think it's time for this little guy to go back into his crate for a bit."

Max's eyes are shining, and I know exactly what he's talking about.

"No more interruptions," I say as I stand with Rocky in my arms. I take him outside so he can relieve himself and then get him settled in his crate. He lets out a little bark but then discovers his chew bone.

When I walk back into the living room, Max is gone.

I frown. "Max?"

"Back here," he calls out from the direction of my bedroom. I hurry back there and smile when I see him leaning his shoulder on the doorframe of my bathroom. "I wanted to see your handiwork."

"Ah." I press my cheek against his back in the groove of his spine and sigh in happiness at his warmth. My arms are wrapped around his middle, pressed against his flat belly.

He's just...*hard.* Firm. Warm.

Irresistible.

"What do you think of it?" I press a kiss to his shoulder blade.

"Just like the rest of the house, it's beautiful."

Claw-foot soaking tub. Subway tile shower. Heated Moroccan tile floor.

I freaking *love* my bathroom.

"I'm glad you like it."

I press another kiss to his back just before he turns in my arms, frames my face in his hands, and lowers his lips to mine.

We're standing in my dark bedroom, kissing as if our lives depend on it.

Over the past week, we've only been able to steal kisses here and there when Alex wasn't looking.

But now, no one is here but us.

The nervousness is gone, and all I want in the world is Max.

"Wills," he whispers against my mouth.

"Yeah."

"I need to get you naked."

I smile because it's the same line he used back in the day when I gave him my virginity.

That was a lifetime ago.

"Okay," I whisper, just as I did back then.

"Are you on the pill?"

"IUD," I reply. "And clean."

"Me, too." His hands glide down my arms, and he links his fingers with mine. "Are you sure about this?"

"I don't think I've ever been more sure of anything in my life."

That line is new and absolutely true.

He smiles softly. He slips his hands under my sweater, skims them up my sides, and pulls the top over my head, tossing it on the floor.

"My body has changed," I warn him.

"So has mine," he says.

"Well, where you've gotten hotter, and thank the good Lord for it, I've had a baby."

"You're amazing," he replies, guiding my jeans down my legs, not worried in the least. Which only makes me love him more because I know, without a doubt, those aren't just pretty words being said to get in my pants.

Max means every syllable.

With my clothes gone, he steps back and takes me in. The light from the bathroom is the only illumination in the room, but it's enough for him to see me.

In the past, I would have moved to cover myself.

But not now.

Not with him.

"Jesus, Wills."

"What?" I glance down and cringe. "I know, these stretch marks are wild. They're not nearly as bad as they were after I first had Alex—"

"No." My gaze whips up to his, and he swallows hard. "No, baby, I was just thinking that I'm going to come faster than an amateur on prom night."

I giggle and step to him, returning the favor of stripping him naked.

My fingers linger over the ridges of his abs. I mean, are these legal in all fifty states? Does he need a license for them? A permit?

A freaking warning label, perhaps?

Max's lips twitch. "Find something you like?"

"I see plenty that I like." My voice is rough with lust. My fingers roam down to the waistband of his jeans. Rather than flick the button open, I run one digit under the fabric, touching his warm skin.

And the tip of his cock.

"That's it," he says, shucking off his jeans, kicking them aside, and lifting me onto the bed.

"I'm sorry, I can't take it. If you keep touching me like that, I'm going to make a fool of myself."

"I *want* to touch you." My hand plunges into his hair as he kisses his way from my neck to my breast, tugging the nipple between his lips. "You're touchable."

"You're fucking incredible," he growls. His mouth devours my breast, and his free hand glides down my belly to home base.

But he doesn't push his fingers inside me or even go straight for my clit.

No, Max Hull lightly brushes his fingertips over my lips on either side of my opening, sending shocks of electricity through every nerve of my body.

"Oh my God," I mutter, my fist tightening in his hair.

"Hold onto the pillow," he instructs me.

I immediately comply. Hell, if he told me to jump off a bridge right now, I'd be swimming with the fishes.

He carefully and methodically plays my pussy like a musical instrument. Taking me right to the edge of reason, then pulling back again until I moan my frustration.

"I need to make sure you're ready," he says.

"I don't think I can get much more ready," I assure him and grin when he nudges his hips between my legs. "Can I let go of the pillow now?"

"You may," he agrees and kisses me deeply. The head of his cock is nestled against me, and as the kiss deepens, it slides farther inside until Max groans and buries his face against my neck. "Fuck, Wills, you feel so damn good."

"Mm." I shift my hips and grip him, grinning when he groans again. Then all conscious thought leaves when he picks up the pace and sends us both into paradise.

After we've caught our breath, he leaves the bed before I can move and comes back with a warm washcloth to clean us both up, then he crawls into the bed next to me, tugging me into his arms.

My cheek on his chest was always my favorite place to be when we were kids, and it seems that's one thing that hasn't changed.

"I can hear your heart," I whisper.

He kisses my head. "Go to sleep."

***

My phone is ringing.

I sit up, disoriented. I'm in my bed, but Max is with me, and suddenly, the past few hours come rushing back to me.

"Phone," I murmur as Max looks around, searching for it. "It must still be in the living room."

"Got it."

He rushes out and then comes running back with the cell, and I accept the call just before it goes to voicemail.

"Mommy?"

Alex only calls me *Mommy* when something's wrong.

"What's going on, Bubba?"

"I want to come home." His voice is so small it breaks my heart. "Can you come get me?"

"Of course." I glance up to see Max pulling on his jeans. "I'll be there in about twenty minutes, okay? Is Pierce's mom awake?"

"His dad is. He said it was okay to call."

"Okay, Bubba. I'll see you in a few."

"Thanks, Mom."

I hang up and blow out a breath.

"Well, so much for a whole night alone," I say, apology in my voice.

"Don't even worry about it," Max assures me as I climb from the bed and pull on a fresh pair of leggings and a baggy sweatshirt. "Let's go get him."

"Oh, you don't have to—"

"If you think I'm going to let you drive alone at two in the morning, you've got another thing coming." He holds his hand out for mine. "Come on. I'll drive."

We hurry out to his Mercedes, and by the time we reach the end of my road, my seat and the air blowing on me are warm.

"This really is a nice car."

He smiles over at me. "You really are beautiful."

He kisses my hand as I blush in the passenger seat. I feel giddy. And, if I'm honest, a little sore.

Now I have to figure out how to tell Max that he can't stay the night once Alex gets home. It's never been an issue with men I've dated in the past because I never let them meet my son. No way.

But this is so different. Not only has Max already met Alex, they genuinely enjoy each other.

I'm not ready for a sleepover and all of the explanations that come with it.

Max pulls into Pierce's driveway, and I immediately jump out and walk to the front door, which is already open with Alex coming outside, a smile on his sweet face at the sight of me.

"Hi, Mom!"

As if it's not two in the morning.

"Hey, Bubba. Go get in the car, and I'll be right there, okay? And what do you say?"

"Thanks for letting me stay. Sorry, I'm a pain in the butt." He waves and hurries down to Max's car, and I roll my eyes.

"I'm sorry about this."

"Hey, it's no big deal," Stan, Pierce's dad, says. "They're at a tough age. They want to feel independent, but they're just not quite brave enough yet. We'll try again in a few months."

"You're the best. Thank you."

I walk back to the car and climb in.

"—weird noises."

"What's that?" I ask.

"Alex was just telling me that there were weird noises."

"Yeah," Alex says. "And it smells funny. Pierce said his mom likes seasonal oils, and he has a water thingy in his room with the oils."

"Essential oils?" I ask with a smile.

"Yeah, that. I didn't like it. I'm sorry, Mom. I know I promised that I'd stay the whole night."

"It's okay." I sigh, sinking back against the warm seat. "We'll try again another time."

"Did Rocky miss me?"

And there it is. The real reason Alex wanted to come home. I should have realized.

"Of course, he did," I reply with a yawn. "Right to bed when we get home, though. It's about three years past your bedtime."

"Can I take Rocky with me?"

"Yeah."

I'm too tired to argue.

By the time we reach my house, I'm ready to head back to bed myself. Max escorts us inside, and I'm faced with the uncomfortable talk.

Alex takes Rocky out of his crate and carries him to bed. I turn to Max, but his hand is already on the doorknob.

"I'll see you tomorrow," he says.

"I'm sorry." I walk into his arms. "This was supposed to be different."

"You're a mom," he says simply. "Sleep well. I'll come over in the morning for breakfast."

"You don't have to—"

He shuts me up with his lips on mine. "I'll see you at breakfast."

And then he's gone.

I walk down the hall to my room, which is two doors down from Alex's. He's in bed, Rocky curled up with him, and he's whispering to his pup.

"I'm glad I came home," he says. "It's fun at Pierce's, but you weren't there, and I missed you. And Mom, but don't tell her that 'cause she might not let me go again, okay?"

I grin and keep walking.

***

"Max is here," Alex announces, the way he always does when he sees Max's car pull into the driveway. "Why was he here last night?"

I was hoping he would forget about that.

"We were on a date."

It's not a lie, and much to my relief, Alex just shrugs and goes back to watching *American Ninja Warrior*.

"Hey," I say as I open the door, then feel my eyes bug out of my face. "What's this?"

"I didn't know what you liked," Max says as he carries four bags to the kitchen and sets them on the island. "Alex, come get breakfast."

"Holy cow!" Alex exclaims at the sight of the bags.

"Holy cow is right," I agree. "What's in here?"

"This bag is bagels and cream cheese. Over here we have omelets and hash browns. I got biscuits with a side of gravy, some fruit, some sausage, and a whole thing of bacon."

Max wiggles his eyebrows.

"The bacon's for me."

"Will you share with me?" Alex asks as he pets Rocky, who's also excited by the smells coming from the bags.

"Sure. One piece."

Alex giggles. "I want an omelet."

"Omelet coming up. With one slice of bacon." Max slaps about four strips of bacon on Alex's plate and winks at me. "What about you, beautiful lady?"

"Just a bagel for me."

"More for us, right, buddy?"

"Yay, more for us!"

CHAPTER EIGHT

Max

I'M RESTLESS.

Work isn't holding my attention, which doesn't usually happen. I just can't get my mind off Willa and Alex. I find my mind wandering, curious about how Alex's math test went today, and what Willa's wearing to work or if she needs help with the puppy.

I have it bad.

And it's interfering with my productivity.

Not good.

It's only been a few days since our interrupted night alone, the best sex of my life, and a fun breakfast the next morning. We spent all day inside, watching movies and the snowfall outside. We made homemade pizza and laughed when Alex spilled his pepperoni on the floor, and Rocky ate it all.

I had no idea that being domesticated could be so fun.

I shake my head as I turn down Noah King's driveway. He lives next door to his birds of prey sanctuary. I pull into his circular drive and hop out of the vehicle. Before I can ring the bell, I hear a loud crack from the side of the house.

I crunch through the snow and find Noah busy chopping firewood.

Thwack!

"Hey," I say, but he doesn't look up. He has earbuds in.

So, like the good friend I am, I scoop up a big ball of fresh snow and hurl it at him, hitting him square in the back. He jerks around, his ax raised high and yanks his earbuds from his head.

"Hello," I say calmly.

"What the hell?" He scowls and reaches to brush at some snow that snuck down his jacket.

"I had to get your attention," I say with a shrug.

"What's up?"

"Not much." I zip my jacket and tuck my hands into my jeans' pockets. It's damn cold out today. Spring should be around the corner, but winter is hanging on like a dog with a bone. "Thought I'd drop by."

"Well, then that means you can chop wood. There are gloves and an extra ax inside the garage."

I nod and go and fetch the gloves and ax. I

like physical work. I sit behind a desk for so many hours at a time that hard work like chopping wood feels good.

When I return, Noah has set up an extra stump for me to chop on. I reach for a piece of wood, steady it on the stump, and *thwack*, chop it in half.

"So, what's really up?" Noah asks, lightly panting. Aside from Cary, Noah and Gray have been my best friends since I was a kid. Noah doesn't mince words. If he sees bullshit, he'll call bullshit. He's loyal, almost to a fault, and one of the smartest guys I know.

I trust his judgment, and I know that anything I say will stay between us.

"I've had a lot on my mind," I begin before setting up another piece of wood to chop.

"Does it have boobs?" he asks, a smile on his damn face.

"Nice ones," I confirm. "And if you look at them again, I'll chop your arm off."

"It's not like I'm leering at them," he points out. "I'm not creepy."

I laugh and stack the wood I've cut so far under the lean-to on the side of Noah's house. He bought it from his parents a few years ago and has made some improvements to the place. He and Gray did most of the work themselves since Gray owns a successful construction company.

"How is Willa?" Noah asks, joining me to stack his firewood.

"She's amazing," I reply immediately.

"So, things are working out then?"

"So far, so good." I nod and walk back to my ax.

"I'm glad," he says, his voice earnest now. "I'm glad you finally pulled your head out of your ass and *did something*."

"But how do you really feel?" My voice is dry as sandpaper.

"You both deserve to be happy, and being together makes you happy." He chops more wood. "When do Brad and Hannah come home?"

"Tonight." *Thwack!* "I'm glad. If you tell him I said this, I'll deny it, but I've missed having Brad around."

"Aw, that's sweet."

I glare at Noah as he laughs and contemplate throwing my ax at him.

"We're having family dinner tomorrow at my place. Kind of a welcome home thing since Jenna and Christian are here, too."

"Is Willa going?"

I frown. "I haven't told her yet, but of course, she's coming."

Noah stares at me as if I just grew a second nose. "Dude, you need to give her notice for these things so she can get a babysitter."

"Why would she need a babysitter? Alex will

come, too."

"So, you've fallen for the kid, too."

"You know, you're kind of pissing me off."

Noah sighs. "I'm not trying to piss you off, I'm just getting a feel for things. You're one of my best friends, and I love you, but you've hurt her before. The rest of us were here to pick up those pieces. Now, it's not just her to worry about. I'm just clarifying that you understand that she's a package deal."

"I'm not a jerk," I reply. "And I don't know who she's dated in the past, but I'm not some idiot who thinks he can date a mom and *not* consider her kids."

"Good."

"I mean, Alex is amazing. I'd challenge anyone to spend just fifteen minutes with that boy and *not* fall in love with him. He's hilarious and smart. Not to mention, cute."

I glance up to find Noah grinning at me.

"What?"

"So, you love him then?"

I swallow and stare over Noah's shoulder, then give a brisk nod. "Of course, I do. I've been in love with Willa since before I really knew what that meant, and Alex is fantastic. I *like* spending time with him. I don't resent it."

"I'm happy for you, man," Noah says, slapping my shoulder. "I really am."

I nod and take another deep breath. "I haven't told her. Somehow, I think saying the words is too big right now. I want her to *believe* them, you know?"

"Willa always was one to guard herself," he says with a nod. "Actions speak way louder than words. You may not have said it, but I'm sure she can feel it."

I hope so.

"Thanks, man." I check the time. "I have to run. Is it okay if I leave you with this?"

"I'd already planned to do it without you. Thanks for the help."

"Anytime. I mean that. It feels good."

"Well, come back in three days. I'll have plenty for you to cut."

"I'll pencil it in."

***

It's become a routine. Every afternoon when Alex gets out of school, I swing into Dress It Up to help the boy with homework and check in on Willa. I crave her, and by the afternoon, I *need* to see her more than I need my next breath.

Today, I walk into the store with a grocery bag dangling from my hand and a latte in the other.

"Hey," Willa says with a bright smile when she sees me approach the counter. "How has your day been?"

"Not bad," I reply, holding the latte out for her.

"Something to warm you up."

"You're sweet," she murmurs, then takes a sip of her drink. "Thank you."

"Is Alex here?"

"He just got here. He took Rocky to the office with him."

I nod, but before I walk to the back, I sneak behind the counter and bury my face in her neck, breathing her in.

"Missed you today," I whisper.

"I'm right here," she whispers back.

"Missed you all the same." I pull back and smile down into her gorgeous face. "Hey, I'm hosting family dinner tomorrow at my place. Brad and Hannah are coming home today."

"I know, I texted Hannah this morning."

"Will you and Alex come?"

She bites her lip and nods. "Of course. Do you want me to cook?"

"No." I scowl and squeeze her hand. "I want you to come and eat good food and hang out with my family. No cooking required."

I plant a quick kiss on her lips, then pull away to walk back to the office. Alex is at his desk, but he's not working on schoolwork. No, he's teaching Rocky tricks.

"Sit," he instructs, but the puppy bounces up to lick his face. Alex giggles. "No, silly. You're supposed to sit."

He puts Rocky on his back haunches and re-peats, "Sit. Good boy."

Rocky gobbles up the offered treat.

"This doesn't look like math," I say, grinning when Alex looks up in surprise. "How was school?"

"Dumb," he grumbles.

"Why was it dumb?"

I sit next to him and set the bag of groceries on Willa's desk.

"Because kids are mean."

I nod. Man, no truer words. But I swear to God, if someone's been shitty to this kid, I will bring hellfire down on that school.

And pull my funding.

"Was someone mean to you today?"

Alex shrugs his little shoulders and pets Rocky, who's curled up in his lap.

"Some kids said I was a geek." He looks up at me. "Have you ever been called a geek?"

"Sure," I say with a nod, relieved that it's this and not something way worse. Not that being called names is okay, but I've heard horror stories from my friends about their kids being bullied. "I mean, you're talking to the guy who works on a computer all the time."

"But what you do is cool," Alex says.

"Why did they say you're a geek?"

"Because I like *Star Wars* and I like to build stuff. And I didn't want to go outside to play soccer. We could choose between that or staying inside to read, and I wanted to read."

"I don't blame you, it's darn cold outside today."

"Yeah, and I'm reading a cool *Goosebumps* book that I got for my birthday. But then they said I was being a geek."

"Well, I think that all of those things sound great, and if that's what being a geek is, then I guess I'm a geek, too."

Alex smiles softly. "Yeah?"

"Absolutely. Maybe those kids are jealous because they don't read as well as you."

He thinks that over as he pets his puppy.

"Maybe," he finally says. "But I wouldn't say bad stuff to them just because they don't read good."

"No, you wouldn't." I ruffle his hair. I want to pull him to me for a big hug, but I don't want to cross any lines. It's still early for all of us. "Because you're a good kid."

"I guess it's good that I like to read. Mom says it is."

"Your mom's smart," I reply with a nod. "And I agree. Reading is very good."

He nods again. "Okay. I just wish they wouldn't laugh and stuff. They're just...dumb."

"That behavior is dumb. And now you know how it feels, so you won't ever treat anyone else that way."

"No, I won't do that."

I pull the pretzel sticks, peanut butter, and hummus out of the grocery bag and get ready to change the subject.

"What's that for?" Alex asks.

"It's to snack on while we do math. I had an idea on how to help with division."

We settle in, working on the problems, using the sticks. They're great as visual aids to help Alex grasp the idea.

"Do you want peanut butter or hummus?" I ask.

He scowls at me. "I'm nine, not forty. I don't want hummus."

I snort, then do my best to look offended. "Hey, I'm not forty."

"Are you my mom's age?"

"I'm a year older than her."

"See?" Alex crunches on a stick. "Old."

"That's the last time I bring in snacks," I reply, making him laugh. Alex takes a bite of his pretzel, then offers the rest to Rocky, who snatches it right up.

"Hi, guys," Willa says, poking her head in. "How's it going back here?"

"Good," Alex responds. "We have snacks."

"Mm, pretzel sticks." She reaches out to grab some, but I shake my head.

"Are you doing math?"

She arches an eyebrow in that way that makes my dick twitch. Way inappropriate around the boy. "Not at the moment."

"Then no pretzels for you. This is math food."

"Did you get him to eat hummus?"

"Heck, no," Alex says, shaking his head. "That's old-people food."

"I like hummus," Willa says.

"I rest my case," Alex responds, making us all laugh.

"Okay, then." Willa watches her son offer a pretzel to Rocky. "No more of those for the baby, Alex. Too much people food upsets his tummy, remember?"

"Yes, ma'am."

Willa leaves the room before Alex rolls his eyes.

"It's just a pretzel."

"And she's your mom, kiddo. You gotta do what she says."

He sighs dramatically. "Fine."

"Do you have this handled for a few? I need to go talk to your mom about something."

"Are you going to tell her about school?" He hangs his head.

"Look at me." He complies, and the worry in his brown eyes tugs at my cold heart. "Unless you're in danger for some reason, I won't tell your mom anything you don't want me to. I promise. Okay?"

He nods. "Okay."

"But if the bullying from these kids gets *any* worse, you need to tell her. She will want to help you, Alex."

"I know. She just worries a lot, and I know that she cries sometimes, too. Or, she did before you started hanging around. And I don't want to make her worry anymore."

"You're a good person, Alex, and I'm lucky to know you."

He smiles proudly as I pat his shoulder, then I set off, looking for Willa.

I find her in the back of the store by the dressing rooms, fidgeting with a rack of dresses.

I wrap my arms around her waist and pull her into a cubicle, then close the curtain and pin her against the wall, kissing the hell out of her.

She's soft and small and smells like sunshine.

She buries her hands in my hair, holding on tightly as I brush my lips over hers, our tongues tangling. I can't help but grind against her, making us both moan.

"Shh," she says with a giggle. "We might not want to do this here."

"I couldn't help myself," I reply, kissing my way down her cheek to her ear. I pull the lobe—earring and all—into my mouth.

"I have a confession."

"If it's another man, I'll kill him," I growl, but she just laughs again.

"No." She rolls her eyes, just like her son, and it makes me smile. "Seeing you help my son is damn sexy."

I feel my lips twitch. "Is that so?"

"Oh, yeah. It's nice that we get along well, and the chemistry is good—"

"*Good*?" I grind myself against her again. "Try fucking amazing."

"…but knowing that you also like my son? Well, that's sexy on a whole new level."

"I'm going to remember this," I promise her.

"Of course, you will."

***

I'm sitting on the lake. It's frozen over, and I have my fishing pole, with the line dropped into the hole in the ice. I'm sitting in a chair, hot coffee in my mug, a blanket on my lap.

The sun is high over me, which is unusual for winter, but I'm happy for the light.

"Nice day," Cary says beside me.

"Cold as fuck," I reply. "But the sun feels good."

"Didn't think this lake would ever freeze over this year," he says, and I nod in agreement. "So, let's get to why I'm here."

"I invited you here," I remind him, but he just smiles, and I realize that he's in shorts and a T-shirt. The same T-shirt he wore every day for a year our junior year. "Dude, you're going to freeze. Where's your coat?"

"One of the cool things about being dead is you don't need a coat."

I scowl as it all comes rushing back to me. The mountain. The snow. Not being able to save Cary.

"I'm sorry," I say, the way I always do when Cary visits me in dreams. "I'm so sorry."

"Not your fault," he reminds me with a sigh and shrugs. "I was dumb."

"Is it really you talking to us when the train whistle blows at your grave? I've been wondering for years."

"Of course," he says with a wink. "I talk to you a lot. You just don't always listen."

"I'll be more aware now." My line tugs, signaling a fish on the other end, and I wrestle with it, finally pulling it out of the water. Cary is waiting with the net. "Thanks, man."

"I miss fishing," he admits.

"What else do you miss?"

He smiles. "Your mama's fried chicken."

"Hell, I miss that," I say with a laugh. "I'll

have to request it the next time I see her."

"I miss my wife." He stresses the my, and the smile falls from his lips. "My son."

"They miss you, too."

He tips his head to the side, and the sun disappears behind clouds. It gets even colder than it was before.

"It's awfully convenient of you to worm your way into my spot there, don't you think?"

"I'm not worming my way anywhere."

"I'm out of the picture, and now you can take over my life? Maybe you pushed me into that tree well on purpose."

"Fuck you," I roar, standing from my chair and flipping it over. "You know that's a load of bullshit."

"And now you're trying to be a daddy to my son. What, just because you're loaded, you think you can be a better dad than me?"

"You're not here," I remind him. "And you were always jealous that Willa had eyes for me. That she was my girl first. Funny how as soon as I left town, you poached her."

"That's right," he says with a smug smile. "And she fell for it, hook, line, and sinker."

"You're a dick."

"Like looking in a mirror, ain't it? So what, are you gonna marry her? Adopt my kid?"

"If I want to."

"Just remember, I was there first. I'm Alex's daddy. And at the end of the day, I'm the one Willa wishes was in her bed, in her body, making her moan."

"I'm going to fucking kill you."

I stomp after him, but he disappears. I'm still on the lake, but the ice is broken, floating on a current. There's a whirlpool up ahead, sucking in everything that comes close to it.

I'm going to get swallowed.

I lay down, trying to paddle the other way, but it's no use. I'm spinning now, hurtling out of control.

BEEP! BEEP! BEEP!

My alarm is going off, pulling me out of the worst nightmare of my life.

And I've had some doozies.

I rub my hands down my face and pad into the bathroom to start the shower. I'm covered in sweat.

And I can't get warm.

CHAPTER NINE

Max

"**Y**OU HEARD ME, I'm coming to Seattle." I stand before my tall windows, staring out at the lake as the caterers hustle behind me, getting dinner set out for my family, who should be arriving anytime. "I'll be in the office tomorrow. I need you to get the house open for me and arrange for the plane to be ready to go at six mountain time in the morning."

"Will do," Charles, my assistant, says. He's been with me for about five years now. He works from Seattle where my main office is but can commute anywhere I need him at a moment's notice. Since I sold a lot of the company, I rarely need him with me these days.

I have some new ideas brewing, however.

"Need anything else?" he asks.

"I'll text if I think of anything," I reply. "See

you tomorrow."

I end the call and turn in time to see Celia, the manager of Ciao, walking toward me with a clipboard. Celia is young and smart and runs a tight ship.

"I think everything's set," she says with a smile. "I just need a signature here."

I don't even glance at the bottom line, I just sign my name and pass it back to her. "Thanks for everything. It smells amazing."

"It's our pleasure, as always."

She marches out with her team of three that came to help. They were in and out in twenty minutes.

I ordered three pans of lasagna, salad, and a massive amount of garlic bread. It'll most likely be too much food, but I won't have to worry about anyone leaving hungry.

I've been off all day. That's the only way I can describe it. The dream freaked me out, even though I know it's only a dream. It wasn't real. Cary didn't visit me to tell me that I'm a son of a bitch for having feelings for his wife and kid.

I *know* that.

But I feel guilty and weird all the same. So, it's time to get away for a few days. Bury myself in some work, take a deep breath, and think.

I've already pulled out my overnight bag. I only take a few things with me since I have a home there with everything I need.

The doorbell rings, and I pull the door open to find Alex and Willa smiling at me. It's like a stab to the heart.

"Your house is *so big*," Alex says as he rushes past me inside, making me grin.

"Hello to you, too," I say as Willa joins me, and I shut the door.

"It's, like, huge," Alex says, running to the windows and looking outside. "Mom! Look at the lake."

"I see it, buddy." She looks at me and shrugs. "We need to get out more."

"It hadn't occurred to me that he hasn't been here before," I admit. We always spend our time together at Willa's house.

"What else is in here?" Alex asks eagerly.

"Alex," Willa admonishes. "Don't forget your manners."

"Sorry," he says. "But really, what else is there?"

"I think we have a minute to show you around," I say with a laugh and take the two of them on a quick trip through all ten thousand square feet.

"You have ping-pong," Alex says, jumping up and down.

"And a movie theater," I say, opening the door to the room in question and flipping on the lights. Alex walks in and stares, struck speechless.

"Whoa. Mom, did you know about this?"

"Yes, I did."

"And you didn't tell me?" Alex looks betrayed as he takes in each of the posters, the popcorn machine, the candy counter. "It's like the real thing."

"I like movies," I say.

"Do you have *Star Wars*?"

"I sure do."

He turns to me with wide eyes. "Can we *please* watch it later?"

"If your mom says it's okay, I'll put it on after dinner for you."

He turns to his mom. "Please, Mom? It's my most favoritest movie!"

"It's fine with me."

"Yesssss!" He pumps his fist in the air and follows us back upstairs to the main level. Willa stops on the stairs in front of me and wraps her arms around my neck, hugging me close. I stiffen for just a second, then return the embrace.

"I missed you today," she whispers.

"How was your day?" I ask. She leans back, her eyes narrowed and watching me closely. There's no way she can tell that anything's up. I'm acting completely normal.

"It was fine," she says. "Are you okay?"

"I'm great," I reply with a smile and gesture for her to keep climbing the stairs. "I think I hear voices up there with Alex."

But she doesn't move. She just cups my cheek, and I immediately feel like a jerk. "Are you sure nothing's bothering you?"

"I'm great," I repeat and lean in to press a quick kiss to her lips. Finally, she turns to lead me upstairs.

"Alex was just telling me that we get to watch *Star Wars* after dinner," Jenna says when we come into the kitchen. "Please tell me he's not lying."

"Looks like it's a movie night," I confirm, and Jenna and Alex exchange a fist bump.

"Awesome," Christian says from behind the island where he's sniffing at the lasagna. "Alex needs to hang out with us more often. We'll have way more movie nights."

"I can do that," Alex says with a nod.

"They're here!" Willa exclaims when the doorbell rings. She runs to answer it, then throws her arms around Hannah. "Oh my gosh, I'm so happy to see you."

"We were only gone for two weeks," Brad says with a smile before wrapping her in a hug.

"That's a long time," Willa says as she closes the door behind them. "Look how tan you both are. I'm so jealous. By this time of year, I'm white as a ghost. I don't remember what the sun looks like."

"You're always welcome to use my house in L.A.," Christian offers, and I suddenly feel defensive, which is stupid.

"I also have a place down that way," I add calmly. "Dinner's on, guys. Help yourselves."

"I love it when Max hosts dinners," Jenna says with a wink. "We get something delicious, *and* I don't have to cook."

"I do my part," I reply with a laugh. Willa steps over to me and links her fingers with mine, then squeezes my hand. I press back. The reassurance that she's here because she *wants to be* is a balm to my soul today.

So why am I trying to back away?

Good question.

My gaze finds Brad's. He cocks a brow.

"You've been gone a while," I say simply.

"Not that long. And I had a signal on my phone."

I shrug. "We'll catch up."

"I want to hear all about the honeymoon," Willa says.

"Ugh, romance," Alex says, sticking his tongue out and making us all laugh.

"That's right, romance is gross." Christian ruffles his hair before offering him some garlic bread. "Just remember that in about six years."

"Thirty years," Willa mutters.

"Go ahead, rub it in that you got to wear your summer clothes and swim in the ocean," Jenna says, and we all take a place at my dining room table. This calms me a bit. My family gathered around, talking about normal things.

I can do this.

"I actually *did* swim in the ocean," Hannah says. "Which I know is a shocker, given that I'm afraid of literally everything."

"She was amazing," Brad adds.

"I'll never do it again," Hannah continues. "I saw a shark. A freaking shark."

"That's *so cool*," Alex says, and I nod in agreement.

"No. It was scary. I don't want to die. So, while it was maybe the most amazing thing I've seen, I don't need to repeat the experience. But it was seriously beautiful there. We sat on the beach or by the pool for a little while every day. Someone was always bringing us a drink or food of some kind."

"That doesn't suck," Willa says.

"There were lots of walks on the beach, and the staff at our resort was amazing. They drew us rose baths every night with lit candles and fruit. It was *so* romantic."

"So jealous," Jenna says with a happy sigh. "And so happy for you. It sounds wonderful."

"I'd like to go back," Brad says with a nod. "Maybe for an anniversary."

"Sooner, rather than later," Hannah agrees. "We highly recommend it. So, what's been going on here?" She glances at Willa and me, and I stuff some bread into my mouth.

"It was my birthday," Alex announces. God, I love that kid. He's so happy, and not afraid to talk. I've never understood the whole *children should be seen and not heard* thing. Alex has good things to say.

"Happy belated birthday," Hannah says. "How did you celebrate?"

Alex happily gives a play-by-play of his party and going to pick up Rocky, not leaving out even one detail.

He could easily fight crime with how well he remembers details.

Having finished my dinner, I stand to start some clean-up. Willa joins me as I toss some aluminum foil into the recycling bin.

"He loves talking about that dog," she says with a grin.

"Of course, he does, it's his favorite thing," I reply. Jenna brings her plate in, and slowly the others filter into the kitchen, as well, each finished with their meals.

"I'm ready for a movie," Jenna says. "Alex, want to come with me and get it queued up?"

"Heck, yes," he says, darting for the stairs. "Last one down is a rotten egg!"

"I don't want to be a rotten egg," Brad says, making a break for the door. Hannah and Christian follow, and then it's just Willa and me left in the kitchen.

"Those jerks left all the dishes for us," I grumble, glaring at the stairs.

"It's fine," Willa says. "You can go with them, and I'll finish this."

"Nah, you go," I reply, shaking my head. "This won't take long."

"Okay," she says, but I can tell by her tone that she's not agreeing to go downstairs. No, that *okay* was the equivalent to *"we need to talk."*

I take a deep breath.

"What's going on with you?" she asks, her hands on her hips. "Because I've sat here for the last hour wondering what I did or said to make you mad at me. Now, I've decided, fuck that, you need to talk to me."

"You haven't done anything wrong." And that's the God's honest truth. This is all me and my own junk.

But I'm not ready to talk about it.

"Okay, then what?"

I sigh and drag my hand down my face. "I need to leave tomorrow. For Seattle."

She takes a step back in retreat, and her face falls, going stark white.

"For good?" Her voice trembles.

"No." I shake my head and pull her into my

arms. God, I'm fucking all of this up. "No, Wills, just for a few days. For work."

Lying to Willa doesn't sit well with me.

It seems *nothing* sits well with me today.

"So, are you being a dick because you're leaving tomorrow, or are you being a dick because you don't want to see me anymore?"

"I'm not being a dick." I frown and step back. She crosses her arms over her chest and scowls.

"Yeah. You are. Trust me, I know dickery, and this is it. So, which is it?"

"I'm not trying to be a dick," I insist. "And I don't want to stop seeing you."

"So you're being a dick—"

"Use a different word, please."

"—jerk because you're going away for a few days? I call bullshit."

I blow out a breath and pace away. I should know better. Willa calls 'em like she sees 'em.

"I'm just moody today," I say at last because that, at least, is the truth. "I have a lot on my mind, and I'm shitty company. If we hadn't already planned this with the family days ago, I would have bailed."

"You can tell me about it," she offers and comes to me again, taking my hand in hers to give it a squeeze. "Sometimes, I'm good at figuring things out."

"Yeah." I sigh and tip my forehead against hers. "I'll tell you about it after I get my own head wrapped around it."

"Promise?"

"I promise."

***

The dreams follow me no matter where I go. Montana or Seattle, it doesn't matter. I've had similar nightmares every damn night.

It's fucking with me.

So what the fuck am I doing here?

I stare at the ceiling, afraid to go back to sleep, and pissed off at Cary for messing with me in my dreams. If that is, in fact, what's happening.

Maybe it's not him at all, but my own garbage.

And if it's happening no matter what, why am I in Seattle, six hundred miles away from the woman I love rather than with *her*? Talking to her? Letting her help me?

I'm a smart man. We haven't said the words, but I know she loves me. And I love her too, more than I ever thought I could love another person.

And I'm doing a stellar job of pushing her away.

Fucking ridiculous.

I thought I needed room to breathe, to put everything in perspective and remember that I'm not poaching on anything. Cary's long dead, and I gave

Willa all the space in the world.

Literally.

Fate wants us together.

I drag my hands through my hair and sit up, then pad down the stairs to the kitchen and open a bottle of water. This house is much, much smaller than my Montana home, but it's comfortable and has amazing views.

It's also empty.

Aside from ghosts that won't leave me the hell alone.

I don't want to hurt Willa. That's the last thing I ever wanted to do, and I could see by the look on her face the other day when I told her I was leaving town that she still has scars from all those years ago.

I hurt her worse than I ever realized.

She's right, I *am* a dick.

She deserves so much better than that. She deserves *everything*. So does Alex. He's such a sweet soul, so loving and generous.

I want to wrap them both up and keep them safe from everything, always.

Cary—or my subconscious—is wrong. I *am* what's best for them, and they're absolutely what's best in my life. The money, the homes, the celebrity? None of that matters if I don't have them with me.

I'm done hurting Willa, and myself. I'm done

standing back, worried about what Cary might think of it. Yes, he was my friend, and I respected him. But he's gone, and Willa and I are alive.

Wasting even one more minute isn't an option.

I pick up my phone and text Charles.

Going back to Cunningham Falls this afternoon. Please have the plane ready by 4:00 p.m.

I check the time. It's after three in the morning, so I don't expect an answer until around seven.

I'll finish up some work here, take a lunch meeting, then head home where I should be.

I never should have left.

CHAPTER TEN

Willa

S*HINE BRIGHT LIKE A DIAMOND.*
I'm singing. Loudly.

Shine bright like a diamond...

And dancing with Jenna, Hannah, and Nina. Dancing my ass off at a bar called Lacey's, where the DJ is playing all of our favorite songs. Alcohol is already moving happily through my veins, and my friends are smiling.

Screw Max and his moodiness. All a girl needs are her friends and some martinis.

"Wooooo!" Jenna is a woo girl. Always has been, especially when she's a bit inebriated.

The song ends, and we sashay our way back to our table. It's in the corner, as far from the music as possible so we can chat.

"How can you wear those shoes and dance?" Hannah asks as I sit next to her.

"I'm used to them now," I reply, glancing down at my four-inch heels. "By the time I get home, my feet will be killing me."

"Liquor helps to cover the pain," Nina reminds us and holds her drink out for all of us to clink. "By the way, you always look so adorable, Willa. Do you have that outfit in your store?"

"Every single piece of it," I confirm with a wink.

"I'll be in tomorrow," Nina says. "I need some wintery things. I have to adjust to this cold climate now that I'm an official resident of Cunningham Falls."

"Welcome home, by the way," Jenna tells Nina with a big smile. "I'm so happy you decided to move here permanently."

Nina is Christian's sister and publicist.

"It makes sense," she says with a shrug. "Christian is here more than he's in California these days, and I like it here."

"I'm glad," I add, also toasting her with my Cosmo.

"I was thinking of starting a business here," Nina confides. "I know all about being a personal assistant to the wealthy, and I think there could be a need for that here."

"More and more as we have more wealthy people moving in," Hannah agrees, nodding. "Heck, I think professionals who aren't necessarily wealthy but still need help could use those services."

"I'm talking about things like personal chefs, holiday decorating, errand running, in-home spas, floral services, shopping, small event planning, and more. I have a couple of friends in L.A. who run a similar company there, and they're ready to branch out."

"You're hired."

We turn in unison to find our friend, Grace, standing at the table.

"Sorry I'm late, guys. The baby made a huge mess, and I had to clean it up and get her settled again with Jacob."

Grace is another dear friend of ours, and the wife of Jacob Berkley. He owns the Blacktail Ski Resort and many other businesses in town, including the bar where we're currently having girls' night.

"How are you feeling?" I ask. Grace just had a baby a couple of weeks ago. "I'm surprised you wanted to come out tonight."

"I needed to get out of the house," she says with a sigh. "I'm feeling good. But no liquor for me tonight. I'm breastfeeding."

"I'll have hers," Nina offers, making us laugh.

"I'll hire you to do all of those things," Grace adds as she sheds her coat and asks the server for an iced tea. "I can't get caught up from having the baby. I love her, but man, she's a lot of work."

"It never ends," I agree with a nod.

"Jacob is working a lot of hours with it still being ski season, and having a service like that would be a lifesaver. So, when you're up and running, let me know. I'll keep you busy."

"My first customer," Nina says excitedly and reaches out to give Grace a high-five.

Grace misses, of course. She's the most *un*-graceful person we know.

"Are you going to quit working for Christian?" I ask Nina.

"No, I'll always work for him, but he's fading out of the limelight more and more. He's happy to make his movies, work the press, then go back to being private with Jenna. There aren't any scandals to handle, and I think I'd like to branch out a bit. Besides, the girls coming from L.A. can totally run things if I'm not available."

"Well, congratulations," Jenna says, holding her glass out to Nina. "And thank the good Lord for no scandals."

"You're not kidding," Nina says with a laugh. "Now, I need to catch up on Willa. What's up with you and Max?"

"Wait." Grace turns to me with wide eyes. "What the hell? Why haven't I heard about this before?"

"Because you just had a baby and you've been a hermit," I remind her.

"Well, shit," she grumbles. "Start from the beginning and use all the dirty words."

"I really like you," Nina says to Grace, making her laugh.

I quickly recount the past few weeks, seeing more of Max, all the way through to the other day at his house when he told me that he was leaving.

"He didn't say anything about leaving to me," Jenna says with a frown. "What the hell got up his ass?"

"I don't know." I finish my drink, then flag down the server for another. "It was weird. Why are men so difficult? They always say *we're* the confusing ones, but we're easy."

"All we need is chocolate, a nice bubble bath, and no bullshit," Hannah says with a nod. "Not hard."

"Yes. Exactly."

"Have you heard from him since he left?" Grace asks.

"A couple of texts, but I've left him alone. If he has some shit to figure out, let him figure it out. I'm too old and too damn busy to chase after him."

"Atta girl," Jenna says.

"When does he come home?" Hannah asks.

"No idea."

"Okay, that's bullshit," Nina says, shaking her head. "If you're in a relationship with someone, you don't pull that crap. It's just inconsiderate."

"The whole thing is weird," I insist. "It's like, one day, everything was normal and fine, and he couldn't keep his hands off me. And then the next, he was distant and had to suddenly leave town for work."

"He got scared," Grace says simply, grabbing all of our attention. "Something spooked him, and he ran away."

"But what? I told him he could talk to me."

"Again, men are stubborn and ridiculous," Jenna says. "Especially Max. He'll talk about it when he's ready, but don't let him blow you off. You don't deserve that."

"Yeah." My head is spinning from my third drink. It's nice. "You're right. He doesn't get to ignore me. In fact, I'm gonna text him now."

"Oh, Lord, no." Hannah yanks my phone out of my hand. "No drunk texting. You'll just be embarrassed in the morning."

"She's right," Jenna says. "But call him tomorrow and tell him off. Do it when you're with me, on speakerphone because I want to hear it."

I giggle. "I wonder if very many people ever give him a piece of their mind?"

"Aside from Brad and me, probably not," Jenna says and sips her margarita.

"Well, you can add my name to the list." I hold out my hand for my phone. "I won't call him drunk."

Probably not.

He hurt my feelings and confused me, and I

hate that. So, when Jenna suggested we come out tonight, I jumped at it.

"I love this song!" Hannah jumps up and grabs Jenna's hand. "Come on, you guys."

"I'll stay here with Grace," Nina says, shaking her head. "You go cut a rug."

"Order another round of drinks." I grin as I scoot out of the booth. "And maybe some food to soak them up."

***

I'm not falling-down drunk.

I'm stumble-around-and-giggle drunk.

There's a difference.

My house is quiet and empty. Mom and Ken took Alex and the puppy to their place for the night. Grace just dropped me off, and I'm not sleepy in the least.

I want to talk.

I want to fuck.

I giggle and shuffle out of my shoes, then pad into the kitchen and look for a snack.

I have Ruffles. Those sound amazing.

I crack open the bag and walk into the living room to plop onto the couch and dig in.

And then, with chips stuffed into my mouth, I dial Max's number.

"Hey, Wills."

"Mshhke"

"Uh, what's that?"

I chew and swallow.

"You made a mistake, buddy."

"How's that?"

I picture him leaning back in a chair behind a desk with his white dress shirt unbuttoned. He's got his feet up on the desktop, and a leggy blonde is standing behind him, rubbing her grabby hands over his chest the way they do in movies.

"First of all, tell the blonde to get her hands off of you."

Silence.

See? I knew it.

"Do you have a fever?" he asks at last.

"No, I'm just not stupid," I reply, my words slurring only a little. "And, second, I went out with the girls tonight, and we danced and drank *a lot.* Alex is gone, and I'm home alone. You could have gotten laid, pal."

"Really."

"Oh, yeah. Because when I've been drinking, I get horny. And I would rock your damn world. But, no, you're in *Seattle* with a blond bimbo who's touching your chest, and that pisses me off."

"There's no blonde. Bimbo or otherwise."

"Sure."

"Is that why you think I left town?"

"I dunno." I frown and feel tears threaten. "You just left. And in the movies, there's a blond bimbo with her hands on you."

"You had a lot to drink."

"Lot of good it did me," I pout and stuff another chip into my mouth. "No interruptions, and I don't even get to have sex."

"That's unfortunate."

"Yeah. I shouldn't have called you. It was stupid."

"You should *always* call me. Whenever you want."

"I'm confused," I whisper. "And you hurt my feelings. You don't get sex. I'll go find my vibrator."

I hang up and stumble into the bedroom, pull the box from the top shelf of my closet, and find the toy, but by the time I get ready for bed and climb in, I'm tired, so I put it back in the box.

And my girls' night out fun is washed away by missing Max.

Suddenly, my front door opens and closes, and I spring up in the bed, immediately sober.

"I have a gun!" I shout, wishing fervently that I *really* had a gun.

"Don't shoot."

Max walks into my bedroom, shocking the hell out of me.

"I could have killed you!"

He circles the bed, not afraid in the least.

"Where's your gun?"

"Well, I don't actually have one."

He grins, and it hits me right in the gut.

"Why are you so handsome?" I ask, but he doesn't answer, he just watches me. "No, really. That wasn't rhetorical."

"I missed you," he says and shoves his hands into his pockets. "And I want to climb in that bed with you, but I don't know if I'm welcome."

"Is there really a blond bimbo?"

He narrows his eyes and clenches his jaw, and I have my answer.

"No."

I fold the covers back. "Then you're welcome."

He's not in a suit, or even in a white button-down. He's in a grey Henley and jeans, and he peels them both off quickly, making my mouth water.

We have so much to talk about, but my mind is cloudy, and he's sexy, and I want him. I've missed him, too.

"How many men do I have to kill?"

"No one actually broke in," I remind him, but he laughs and shakes his head as he climbs into the bed with me.

"No, how many men hit on you tonight?"

"None." I drag my hands down his back and sigh in delight when I cup his ass. "I don't give off a come-hit-on-me vibe."

"What kind of vibe do you give off?"

"It's more of an I'm with my friends, and if you hit on me, I'll laugh at you, vibe."

"I can live with that," Max says and buries his face in my neck, kissing me as his hands roam over my skin, seemingly everywhere at once.

"I thought you were gone."

"I came home a few hours ago." He kisses my cheek. "I couldn't stay away any longer."

"Good." I lift my legs as he settles between them, and his hard cock nestles against my wet heat. "Because you belong here."

"Right here," he agrees as he slides back and forth, making me crazy. "And I won't be leaving again unless you're with me."

"Okay." I arch my back, desperate to have him *in* me. "Max, I need—"

"What do you need, baby?"

"You to slip inside me."

He smiles against my lips, rears back, and slowly pushes his way inside until he's buried to the hilt.

"Like that?"

"Yeah." I'm panting now, gripping his shoulders with all my might. I can feel the edge *just* out of my reach. "Move."

"Bossy, aren't you?"

"Needy," I correct him and arch my back again. He complies, moving in and out, slowly at first, then picking up the pace. Each time his pubic bone meets my clit, he gives it a little extra push, and I swear to God my eyes cross.

"Jesus Christ, you feel good," he mutters. He's moving feverishly now, chasing his own orgasm, and I can't control myself anymore. My hips buck, and I cry out as the orgasm washes over me. Max follows, groaning against my neck.

"Wow," I whisper, dragging my fingertips up and down his spine. He's a little sweaty, but I don't mind. I like feeling him on top of me. "That was fun and unexpected."

"I was going to call you just before you called me," he mutters, still catching his breath. "And then you surprised me. Kind of pissed me off, assuming I had another woman with me."

"I was drunk, and my feelings were hurt." I shrug a shoulder and watch as he rolls off me, taking me with him. He tucks me against his side. "And, a girl will overthink everything, especially possible reasons why the guy she's with suddenly gets a hair up his ass to flee town."

"I didn't flee," he counters and slaps my ass. "Now, get some sleep. We'll talk about it in the morning."

I yawn. I want to disagree, to insist that we

talk it out tonight. But I *am* tired, and my eyes are heavy. I want to have this conversation when I have a clear head, and I'm not in a sexual haze of desire.

Tomorrow is definitely the right time to talk it out, and we will. Before my mom brings Alex home. I'll text her in the morning and ask her to keep him until the afternoon.

It feels good to be here with Max. Safe. Like my world is back on its axis again.

I guess Hannah was wrong. I definitely do *not* regret drunk-calling Max tonight. No, it turned out just fine for me.

I stretch against him, kiss his shoulder, and tangle my leg with his.

"Are you too warm?" I ask.

"No, I'm warm for the first time in days. Don't go."

I kiss his shoulder again and burrow deeper. "I'm not going anywhere."

CHAPTER ELEVEN

Willa

"I FEEL HUMAN AGAIN," I announce as I pad down the hallway to the kitchen, where Max is scooping scrambled eggs onto plates. "And I smell bacon."

"I made you breakfast," he says with a smile and leans in for a quick kiss. "Hungover?"

"Not at all." I walk over to the Keurig to brew my second cup of coffee and lean against the counter to watch Max move about my kitchen. He's tall and broad, with his dark hair disheveled, wearing the same clothes from last night.

His feet are bare, and for some reason I can't put my finger on, I find that ridiculously hot.

Of course, *Max* is ridiculously hot.

Every day.

Damn him.

"Do you need ketchup or anything?" he asks.

"Nope."

"Then breakfast is served."

He carries our plates to the breakfast nook that's tucked behind the kitchen. The round table sits before a bay window that looks out into my backyard. Deer walk across the grass.

"Thanks for cooking." I take a bite of bacon and sigh in happiness. "I don't usually get a home-cooked meal that I didn't make myself."

"I'm pretty good at breakfast," Max says with a crooked smile. "The rest of the day isn't as great."

"I can live with that." I sprinkle some pepper on my eggs and take a bite. "So, how was Seattle?"

"It was fine," he says, not meeting my eyes.

"That's good."

I hate this. Awkwardness has never been our thing. I get the feeling that he's not telling me something, but I won't ask him to talk about it again. I've done that. He's an adult. When he's ready to talk, he will.

Or, he won't.

"So, you came home yesterday?" I ask lamely, wanting to fill the silence.

"Yeah, I left Seattle around five Montana time, and it was early evening by the time I got home and settled. I had a little work to see to, and then I was going to call, but you beat me to it."

I nod, a little embarrassed by how I must have sounded when he answered the phone.

"What's wrong?" he asks.

"I'm not usually one to drunk-dial someone."

"You're kidding." His voice is dry, making me laugh.

"I'm actually not one to drink much, period. I have Alex." It's as simple as that, and Max doesn't need me to explain further. He nods.

"But if you're always horny when you're a little drunk, we could probably schedule it in once in a while."

I snicker and take a bite of my eggs. "Trust me, you don't need to get me liquored up for me to want to bang you."

"You're so romantic, darling."

I giggle again. "Wanting you isn't an issue."

"That's a relief."

"As long as there are no blond bimbos."

He narrows his eyes and carefully sets his coffee mug down. Before I can react, he reaches out, grabs my wrist, and tugs me into his lap, then cups my jaw and brushes his thumb along my lower lip.

"There's no one but you, Wills. Haven't you figured that out by now?"

I sigh and tip my forehead down to his before admitting, "I'm not good at feeling insecure."

"I don't like that I made you feel that way," he

says. He swallows, kisses me, then sets me back in my chair. "We need to talk."

This is it. He's dumping me.

"You're blinking."

I glance up at him. "What?"

"You're blinking rapidly. You only do that when you think something bad is going to happen."

And that's the downside to rekindling something with the person who used to know you better than anyone. He knows all your tells.

I never did have a poker face.

"'We need to talk' is not usually something that a person starts with when it's good news. So, if you're breaking it off, just say so."

"Jesus, Willa, I wouldn't come in here, spend the night in your bed, make you breakfast, and *then* dump you."

"So, you're not dumping me?"

He swears under his breath and drags his hand down his face like he does when he's frustrated. A little light of hope ignites in my chest.

"No." He sighs and pushes his half-eaten plate of food away, then cradles his mug in his hands. "But we do need to talk about the past week."

"Go on." I clear my throat and take a sip of my coffee.

"You were right when you said I ran away. I didn't want to admit it, but that's exactly what I did."

"Why?"

His eyes are pinned to mine now, sober and serious.

"I've been dreaming," he says, surprising me.

"Dreaming?"

He nods and sips his coffee, then sets the empty mug aside and looks outside to watch a doe with her baby.

"About Cary. They're nightmares. I've had dreams about Cary, about him dying, since that day on the mountain."

"Max—"

"But these are different."

He goes on to describe the horrible things Cary said to him, accusing him of stealing Alex and me, of killing him so Max could get his hands on us.

My God.

I brush at a tear rolling down my cheek as Max finishes telling me about the last nightmare in Seattle.

"Max, I'm so sorry. I wish you'd told me about this right away."

"I was caught off guard," he admits. "Like I said, I've dreamed about Cary off and on for years, and while they sucked, they weren't hurtful. Not like this. And I didn't know what to do with it. What if he's right?"

I frown as he turns his worried gaze to mine.

"You did *not* kill Cary," I insist.

"No, I know that. But what if he's right about things now? That I'm poaching his family?"

"Max, you need to take a deep breath and think about this. First of all, Cary wouldn't talk to you like that. He had moments of asshattery, but he loved you, and he wouldn't say those things to you.

"Secondly, he's *not here.* You're not poaching on his territory because it's not his. He's gone. Alex and I are happy and *fine.* If you'd rather back out of our lives, don't use this as a reason, because it's completely unnecessary."

"I don't want to back out of your lives," he admits. "I don't think I could if I tried. I was gone for four days, and being away from you drove me insane."

"Well, I kind of like the sound of that," I admit and reach out to take his hand, linking our fingers. "Because I hated that you left. I *need* you to talk to me. Don't back away. Don't flee. Because that just tells me that you don't want to try, and that hurts worse than if you stayed and fought."

"Lesson learned," he says, tugging me back into his arms. "When does Alex come home?"

"In about three hours." I bury my face in the crook of his neck and just hold on tightly, soaking in the scent of him, and the warmth of his arms wrapped tightly around me. "Do you mind running me into town to pick up your car?"

"Why's it in town?"

"Because I didn't plan to drink that much. Grace drove me home."

"I'll take you," he confirms as he stands with me still in his arms and marches back toward my bedroom. "Later."

"Later?"

He tosses me onto the bed, making me laugh, and then strips out of his clothes before climbing on top of me.

"Much later."

***

"Mom, these snow pants are too big around my feet."

I glance into the backseat. "I know, but when you put your boots on, they'll fit fine. You'll see."

"Where are we going again?" Alex asks. He's been in a mood today. Ever since I told him that we couldn't bring Rocky with us on our adventure, his attitude has been crappy.

"We're going out to the King ranch," Max says with a smile. "They have a ton of land, with the best sledding hills around. There will be other kids there, and Noah and Gray, too."

"I haven't seen Jillian and Cara in a while," I say with a smile. "It's always good to hang out with them."

"Do you know them well?" Max asks.

"I know Cara through Grace. They taught school together. And, of course, small-town living means that I've met everyone several times. Cara and Jillian are a few years older than me, but they come to the shop quite a bit, and Jillian is in my yoga class."

Max's eyes whip over to me. "You take yoga?"

"Twice a week," I confirm.

"Huh."

"What?"

He shakes his head but looks over at me with mischief in his eyes, and I know his answer is not suitable for mixed company.

I laugh and feel the heat between my legs at the same time. Max has a habit of turning me on at the oddest moments.

It's been one week since our time alone at my house. We've settled back into a steady rhythm of dinners together, Max bringing me coffee or lunch, and helping Alex with his homework.

It's completely normal, and it feels amazing.

Max turns off the highway about twelve miles out of town and onto the driveway of the Lazy K Ranch. We keep going past a big, old farmhouse where Jillian and her husband, Zack, live with their four children.

Across the pasture, where dozens of black cows are grazing, I can see the smaller house that Zack and Josh's parents moved into several years ago.

And, finally, about another mile in, we reach Josh and Cara's home.

This is a true family ranch, with all hands on deck. Zack returned home about five years ago after retiring from the military. His son, Seth, was already here, living with Josh.

In the past five years, the family has grown like crazy. Cara and Josh have two young kids, both under four years old.

Seth is a junior in high school now, and a mirror image of his father and uncle, who are identical twins.

Zack and Jillian also have three-year-old twins, and another baby on the way any day now.

"Looks like Ty and Lauren are here, too," I say with excitement. "I haven't seen her since she had the new baby."

"There are gonna be babies here?" Alex grumbles.

"Max, can you please give me a moment with my son?"

Max raises a brow but nods as he shuts off the car.

"You bet. Just come inside when you're ready."

"Thanks." Max leaves, and I unbuckle my belt, then turn in my seat so I can look at my son. "What's going on, Alex?"

"Nothing."

"Stop playing with your zipper and look at

me." He complies. "We can't always take Rocky with us."

"But he likes the snow."

"Listen to me. It's not polite to bring a dog to someone else's home, Alex. Rocky can stay home sometimes."

"He'll be sad."

"And then he'll be happy when you get home," I remind him. "Alex, Rocky doesn't run the show. He's a dog, and we love him, but he's still a dog, and sometimes, he doesn't get to go with us."

Alex sighs dramatically, something he's started doing recently. The teen years are going to be a blast, I just know it.

"Fine."

"Excuse me?"

"Yes, ma'am."

"Don't you want to sled?"

"I do," he says reluctantly. "But I want to ski more."

"We've talked about this," I remind him, putting an end to the conversation. "You know how I feel about skiing."

"Yes, ma'am," he grumbles again.

"There will be lots of kids here today, and Max will sled with you, too. I bet Noah and Gray want to sled also."

"Okay," he says.

"Will you please shake the attitude?"

He frowns, but I leave it at that and jump out of the car. I open his door and hold my hand out for his.

"Come on. I bet there're snacks and goodies in there, and we don't want Max to eat them all."

That catches his interest, and he jumps out of the car, then waits patiently as we knock on the door.

Max answers it and searches my face for answers. "Everything okay?"

"Yep."

The King household is a riot of activity. Kids and adults alike, running and laughing, tackling each other. Jillian, even more pregnant than when I saw her at yoga last week, is sitting on the couch, letting Cara's daughter listen with her little ear pressed against the baby bump.

Ty and Lauren are in the kitchen with Jeff King, the patriarch of this family, showing off their littlest.

I'll never remember all of the names, or even who belongs to whom. I just know that it feels amazing to be in the hustle and bustle of this big family.

I always wanted a big family. I have an older brother, Jesse, who I never see. I haven't heard from him in over a year, and we were never especially close to begin with.

Being in the middle of a family like this fills my cup.

"Mom, I think I'm the oldest kid here," Alex whispers up to me, looking mortified.

"Seth is older than you," Max says, pointing to the tall, lanky boy currently playing a video game with his dad.

But Alex is right. He's at an awkward age, with Seth being way older, and the others being way younger than him.

"Hey, Alex," Noah says with a smile. "I want to go sledding. How about you?"

"I guess." My son glances around nervously, and I suddenly wish I'd thought to invite Pierce to come along so Alex would have someone his own age with him.

"I want to go, too," Max says. "I'll go out and get the gear out of the car."

"Same," Seth says, tossing his controller onto the coffee table. "Alex, you can ride on my four-wheeler if you want."

Alex's face whips up to mine, his eyes big and hopeful, and I immediately know that today is going to be just fine.

"Can I, Mom?"

"I don't—"

"I have a helmet for him," Seth assures me, giving me a smile that must have every girl in the high school losing their damn minds. "And I won't go too fast."

"Can I? Can I?"

"Yes, but please be careful."

"You bet," Seth replies and leads Alex out back.

"Alex is safe with Seth," Cara assures me with a serene smile. She's a petite blonde, with curves in all the right places. She's happy and welcoming.

"We got Seth a new four-wheeler for Christmas because he outgrew the last one," Jillian adds. Where Cara is fair, Jillian is dark. The two women are yin and yang, and the best of friends. "He's in an adult size now."

"He's tall," I agree, nodding. "I'd say he's almost as tall as his dad."

"It kills me," Jillian says, shaking her head. "My boy is growing up."

"And he's a good kid," Cara adds as she shifts a child from her hip to a high chair. "We're going to hang out in here with the little ones, but you're welcome to go out with everyone else. Enjoy the sledding for a bit, then come back in here for a hot toddy."

"That actually sounds really good. I never get to play outside. But I bet I'll be tired of it in fifteen minutes."

"I'll have something hot to drink ready for you," Cara assures me. I follow where the guys went, out behind the house where about eight four-wheelers are parked along a fence-line as if they're cars parked at the mall.

"This is interesting."

"In the summer, those are horses," Zack says with a wink.

"You're with me," Max says as he swings a leg over one of the vehicles. "Ready?"

"Hell, yes," I murmur as I climb on behind him and hold on as he drives us through the snow, following the others. The ski hill for today is about a mile from the house, nestled in the trees. The mountains are beautiful, covered in fresh snow.

Noah and Gray have already developed a pull-system, using two of the four-wheelers to pull the kids on their sleds up the hill so they can sled down without having to hike up.

"Seems like cheating," I say to Max, who just shrugs and wraps an arm around my shoulders.

"I don't want to hike up that thing."

"Good point."

"Mom!" Alex calls, waving at me as he's towed up the hill. "Watch me, okay?"

"I'm watching!" I call back. Seth is at the top of the hill and gives Alex instructions before giving him a gentle push down.

"Yeah!" Alex yells as he sails down the hill, but just as he reaches the bottom, he topples off the sled. Assuming he'll pop up with a laugh, we wait.

But he doesn't.

He pops up, gasping for breath, and Max and I run to him. Noah's already there.

"Hey, buddy," Max says, taking Alex by the shoulders. "Calm down and take a deep breath."

"What's going on?" I demand.

"Just got the wind knocked out of him," Noah says with a wink.

"You're okay, Alex," Max croons. "Take another breath."

Finally, Alex breaks down and cries and clings to Max's jacket.

"I know it's scary," Max says and kisses Alex's head, making me swoon. "It totally sucks, but you'll feel better in just a minute."

"I'm done," Alex says, angrily swiping at the alligator tears. "I want to go home."

"You just got here," Seth says as he joins us.

"I'm done," Alex repeats, standing and walking in the direction of the house.

"Alex—" I begin to chastise him, but Max holds up a hand as if to say, "*give me a minute.*"

"That's not how we do this, buddy," Max says, making Alex stop in his tracks. "When you fall, you have to get back up and do it again. Otherwise, you've let the scary thing beat you, and I know you're not a quitter."

Alex frowns, looking down at his boots and then back up at Max.

"Do you think if my dad didn't die, he would have gotten back on the skis?"

I hold my breath, surprised by the question.

No, not surprised.

Shocked.

"Yes, I do," Max says. "He would have gotten right back up and skied down the hill."

Alex thinks about it for a second, then walks back to Noah.

"Okay, I'm ready to go again."

"Let's go, then," Noah says, but looks at both Max and me with sober eyes. He starts the four-wheeler and pulls Alex behind him.

"Well, damn," Zack mutters when Alex is out of earshot.

"He's never asked about his dad like that," I say softly so only Josh, Zack, Ty, and Max can hear me. "Never."

"He's growing up, and he's curious," Josh says.

"And he's around Max more," Ty adds. "Maybe that's making him think more about his dad."

Max and I share a look.

"Just when I thought I had this parenthood thing in the bag," I say, shaking my head.

"It's never in the bag," Zack says with a wink. "Trust me on that."

CHAPTER TWELVE

Max

IM PRETTY SURE I just swallowed my tongue.

Had a heart attack.

Stroke.

Something.

Because, my God, just look at her.

"Are you okay?" Willa asks from inside the door, smiling at me with uncertainty in her brown eyes. "Is this dress not appropriate?"

"It's appropriate for many things," I reply, finally finding my voice and following her into the house and closing the door. "Like lying in a heap around your ankles after I rip it off of you."

"Hey, this was an expensive dress," she says, scowling at me as if she's scolding a child.

Which only turns me on more.

The fabric is ice-blue and shiny, falling in thick, floating cascades, shimmering from her chest to the floor. It molds to her breasts but hides the rest of her, flowing as she walks. Sapphires twinkle at her ears and around her wrist as she reaches for a white fur wrap.

I take it from her and slip it around her shoulders, leaning in to press my lips against her neck, just below a sparkling sapphire.

"You're absolutely stunning," I whisper against her skin. "You take my fucking breath away."

"That's better." She smiles up at me, then turns to adjust my already straight tie. I think it's a woman thing to adjust a man's tie whether it's straight or not. "You're handsome yourself."

"He's in the bath," Debbie says as she comes out of Alex's bathroom. "Oh, hi, Max."

"Hello."

"My goodness, you two look like you should be in a magazine. Here, Willa, give me your phone, and I'll take a picture."

She arranges us in front of the fireplace and snaps a few photos.

"We might be late," Willa warns her, but Debbie just shakes her head and smiles.

"Take all the time you want. The kiddo will be in bed soon. In fact, stay out all night if you like."

"Oh, I don't—" Willa begins, but I cut her off.

"That would be great, if you're sure."

Debbie winks at me. "You got it."

"Ready?" I ask Willa as she grabs her clutch and checks her lipstick in the mirror by the front door.

"Looks like it," she says with a nod.

"Oh, Max," Debbie says before I shut the door behind us. "I think that what you've done for the hospital is just wonderful. Thank you."

"My pleasure." I nod and close the door, then help Willa down the stairs. "Those shoes aren't really appropriate for snow."

"I'm not wearing boots under my dress," she says, holding onto me as she maneuvers her way into the vehicle. "Besides, they'll look fantastic around your shoulders later."

"I—" I swallow hard and try again. "I think we'll skip this fucking party and go straight to my house."

She's still laughing when I climb into the car next to her. "We can't skip a party being thrown in your honor," she says.

"I could say I came down with a case of something."

"Nope." She grins over at me. "I'm dressed for a fancy party, and that's what I want."

"Then a fancy party the lady shall have."

***

"I guess it didn't occur to me that I'd know just about everyone here," Willa says an hour later after saying hello to half of the town. "Then again, I'm not the only one who loves a fancy shindig."

"Didn't you sell a bunch of formal dresses this winter?" Abby, Hannah's cousin, asks.

"I did, actually. I just didn't put two and two together. Math isn't my strong suit."

"I love your dress, Abby," Hannah says, making her cousin blush. "What did I say?"

"This was my backup dress," Abby says, giving her date, Dr. Drake Merritt, the side-eye.

"What happened to the other one? Is it defective? Should I send it back?" Willa asks.

"No, nothing like that," Abby says.

"I ripped the first one off of her," Drake says calmly as if he's discussing the weather.

"*Drake!*" Abby says.

"What? It's the truth."

"Well, at least you had a backup plan," Willa says with a laugh, glancing at me because I had the same exact thought when I saw her earlier.

We're at a table with Brad and Hannah, Abby and Drake, and Jacob and Grace, who are currently across the room chatting with the medical director of the hospital.

"Oh, my phone is ringing." Willa frowns and pulls the cell out of her clutch. "It's not my mom."

"Who is it?" I ask.

"Unknown number. Must be Jesse. Hello?" Her

face lights up, confirming that it's her brother. "You have the worst timing. Well, get a regular phone, and I could text you. ...I know. I'm at a party with some friends, but Mom's at my place with Alex. You should call them. ...Okay, love you, too. Bye."

"How is Jesse?" Brad asks. He and Jesse were in the same grade in school. Jesse went into the military after graduation and has rarely come home since.

"Fine, I think," Willa says as she tucks her phone into her bag. "I don't hear from him much."

"Top-secret maneuvers," Hannah says with a wink. "That's what happens when your brother is 007."

"I don't know what he is, honestly," Willa replies. "He doesn't tell us anything. But he sounded good."

"Ladies and gentlemen, please take your seats." A local celebrity, a radio DJ who has been around for a long time, is the master of ceremonies tonight. In addition to the large donation that Jacob and I made, there's a silent auction happening, and he will reveal the winners after the announcement of the donation. "Before we begin with the silent auction winners—I really hope I won that trip to Maui for my wife and myself—I'd like to invite two men to come up and join me.

"Please give Max Hull and Jacob Berkley a round of applause."

Jacob and I stand, buttoning our coats, and

walk through the ballroom to the podium. We decided beforehand that I would be the one to speak on behalf of both of us.

"Good evening," I begin and wait for the room to quiet. "Jacob and I are honored to be with you tonight. As you know, the money collected from the silent auction benefits the hospital, going toward the new cancer facility set to break ground in the spring.

"It is my distinct privilege to announce that Jacob and I have each donated one million dollars toward this worthy cause."

The room erupts into applause, and I step back to shake Jacob's hand, then look out across the crowd to find Willa, who is beaming proudly. She knew that I was making a donation tonight, but I hadn't told her how much.

Jacob and I smile and pose for a round of photos, then return to our seats with our friends.

"I had no idea," Willa whispers in my ear.

"I know." I take her hand in mine and kiss it, ignoring the looks from those seated near us. Tonight is the first time we've been outwardly affectionate in public, and it already has the rumor mill buzzing.

Let it buzz. I don't give a shit.

Willa's mine. I'd gladly take out a full-page ad in the newspaper if that's what it takes to let everyone know that I'm completely gone over her. Hell, I never *stopped* loving her for the girl she was, and

I can't resist the amazing woman she is now. I'm damn proud to have her by my side.

***

"I'm drowning," Willa says the next morning. She's at the shop, and Alex is out of school. Her mom is helping her, along with the two girls Willa hired as part-time help, but they're barely keeping up.

"Did you make everything free?" I ask, looking around in awe.

"Almost. It's a winter sale so I can make room for the spring inventory I have coming in. Everything's fifty-percent off. Apparently, the advertising I did worked."

"You're a walking advertisement," I remind her, watching as a woman in her early twenties squeals with delight when she finds the pair of jeans she's been looking for. "You always look fantastic, Wills. They just want to look like you."

"They just want a killer deal on a pair of jeans," she says, but boosts herself up on her tiptoes and offers me a kiss. "But thank you for saying sweet things."

"They're true." I kiss her plump lips. "How can I help?"

"I was hoping Alex could spend the day with Ken, but he caught the flu. Ken, not Alex. And I need Mom here—"

"I got this," I say easily as Alex joins us. "I'll take Alex for the day."

"Yes!" Alex exclaims, holding his hand up for a high-five.

"Are you sure? You don't have to do that."

"I'm totally sure."

"What are you going to do?"

"We'll figure it out," I reply with a shrug.

"Yeah, Mom," Alex says, shrugging the same way I just did. "We'll figure it out."

She sighs, looking back and forth between us, and then shrugs herself. "Okay. Thank you. And, Alexander Cary Monroe, you behave and do as you're told. You've had a crappy attitude lately."

"Wow, your full name, dude."

"Yeah," Alex says, staring at the floor. "Yes, ma'am, I'll be good."

She squats in front of him and pulls him in for a hug. "I love you *so much*. You hurt my feelings when you sass me."

"I'm sorry," he says and kisses her cheek. "I'll be good. Honest."

"Okay, then." She smiles up at me as if I hung the moon. I enjoy the kid. If spending time with him earns me looks like that, I'll take him every day. "Have fun."

"We will." I kiss her lips once more, then follow Alex to her office so we can gather his jacket. "Where's Rocky?"

"At Grandma and Grandpa's," he says, moping. "*I* couldn't go because Grandpa's sick, but Rocky got to go."

"I bet he's good company for your grandpa," I say as he shoves his arms into his coat. "I know that it would help me feel better to have a puppy to snuggle."

"Oh." He considers that for a minute, then nods. "Yeah, I guess you're right."

We walk out the back door to avoid the crowded showroom and climb into my car.

"What should we do today?" I ask. "Ice skating? Movie?"

"I want to go skiing," Alex announces proudly. "Can we go?"

"I don't know, Alex." I turn toward my house, expecting to spend the day in the theater with movies for the kiddo and my laptop. "I don't know if your mom would be okay with that."

In fact, I'd be shocked if she *was* okay with it after what happened to Cary.

"She's totally fine with it," he replies easily. "I was supposed to take skiing lessons this year, but we didn't have time. In fact, you'll be doing *her* a favor if you take me 'cause then she won't have to."

I glance over at him, and he looks so sincere and excited, how can I tell him no?

"We don't have your snow pants with you."

"They're in my backpack," he replies. "See?

It's like we were supposed to go skiing today."

"Now you're laying it on a little thick."

"Does this mean we get to go?" he asks hopefully.

"Yes, *but...* You have to stay close to me at all times and do exactly what I say so you don't get hurt. This is important, Alex."

"I will do that," he says, nodding. "Honest. I'll listen."

"If you don't, we'll stop and go home."

"I understand." He's solemn and earnest, so I decide to take the day off with him and spend it doing what I love the most: skiing.

It's crazy that I'm taking my best friend's son skiing for the first time. I wish Cary were here with us. He'd be so excited.

But he's not. I'll keep Alex safe and show him the ropes on the bunny hill today.

The drive up to the resort is quick. I park and help Alex into his snow pants, then slide mine on, as well. I always keep a pair in the car, along with boots, skis, and poles, because I sometimes decide on a whim to come up and ski a run or two.

I won't be using my skis today, so I slide on my snow boots, lock up the car, and take Alex's hand.

"Ready?"

"This is going to be the best thing *ever*," he replies, skipping next to me.

"First, we have to go rent your equipment. If this becomes something that you really like and you want to stay with it, I'll get you your own skis and boots next year."

"You'd do that?" he asks with wide eyes.

"Of course." I ruffle his hair, then hand him his hat. "You'll need this. It's cold up here today."

Thirty minutes later, Alex has skis, boots, and poles, and we're headed for the bunny slopes when I hear someone call my name.

I glance around to find Jacob approaching with someone I don't know at his side.

"Hey, hold up," Jacob says. "I want you to meet my mate, Sebastian. Sebastian, this is Max Hull, a good friend of mine."

"I know the name for certain," Sebastian says with a smile, shaking my hand. His face looks familiar.

"Have we met?" I ask him.

"No, this is my first time in Cunningham Falls, but I'm glad I came. Jacob has been trying to get me to visit for years."

"We went to college together at Oxford," Jacob says as Alex tugs on my sleeve.

"This is Alex Monroe, a friend of mine," I say, introducing Alex to Sebastian. "He's never skied before, so I thought I'd show him the ropes."

"Really?" Jacob frowns, but something from the corner of his eye catches his attention. "Oh, bollocks, I have to run. Sebastian?"

"I'm with you," Sebastian says and smiles at both Alex and me. "Nice to meet you both. I hope to see you again."

He waves and rushes off, and I lead Alex to the chairlift that leads to the simplest run.

"I like their voices," he says with a smile.

"They're British," I inform him.

"I know, I like it. Okay, what do we do first?"

I show him how to hop on and off of the chairlift, which is enough to make him giddy. When we hop off, and I take him through some lessons, he's all smiles, mastering it quickly and efficiently, just like his father.

He does exactly as I say, listening intently and being the perfect student.

When it's time to call it a day, Alex sighs with happiness and walks, slower now, to my car after we hand in his gear.

"This was the best day ever," he says, settling back on the seat. "Like, ever *ever.*"

"You did a great job," I say, easing down the mountain. It snowed while we were skiing and has gotten colder, making the road more treacherous. "I'd say you're a natural."

"Like my dad?" he asks eagerly, and I remember what Willa said the other day about Alex not asking many questions about his dad.

"Absolutely."

"Awesome."

"You know, your dad and I learned to ski to-gether." Memories flood my mind of two little boys as excited as Alex was today to learn to fly down the mountain.

"Really? You knew him that long?"

"Pretty much his whole life," I confirm.

"What was he like?"

I glance at Alex. I feel like I'm treading on thin ice here, but Alex doesn't look sad or upset. It's as if he's asking me what *anyone* is like.

"He was funny. He always had a joke to tell."

"Mom says I'm funny, too," Alex says.

"You probably get that from him, then," I say, nodding. "He liked to fish and go out on the boat. Basically, if it was outside, your dad liked it."

Alex frowns. "What was his favorite movie?"

"Hmm, I'm not sure. He liked *Star Wars*, and he loved action movies. I think *Die Hard* was one of his favorites."

"Mom won't let me watch it, even though Pierce says it's a Christmas movie."

"Well, that just gives you something to look forward to, I guess."

He shrugs a shoulder. "Did he have a dog?"

"Have you ever asked your mom or your nana and papa these questions?"

"No," he says quietly. "I think talking about my

dad makes them sad. Especially Nana and Papa."

"I'm sure they'd be happy to answer your questions," I insist. "It was a long time ago, Alex. And I know that they will always love him, but you have every right to ask questions about him, too."

"Yeah. Nana and Papa are coming to visit next week. Maybe I can ask about him then."

"That's a good idea." My phone rings. "It's your mom."

I accept the call on the Bluetooth.

"Hi, guys," she says happily. "How's it going?"

"Good," we reply in unison. "We're headed back to my house. Unless there's something you need first."

"No, I'm fine, I was just checking in. You're just now headed to your house? Where have you been?"

I glance at Alex, but his eyes are wide, and his skin is whiter than before. I have a very, very bad feeling.

"We went skiing," I reply and watch Alex gulp.

"You did *what*?" Willa demands.

"Uh-oh," Alex whispers.

CHAPTER THIRTEEN

Willa

"I CAN'T BELIEVE THIS," I mutter as I throw my stuff into my handbag, stomping around my office like a caged animal.

"Don't freak out," Mom warns me, watching me pace. "You don't know the whole story."

"They went *skiing.* That's all I need to know. I can't believe I trusted him."

"Should I drive you home?"

I glance over to find Mom scowling in concern. "No. I'm fine. Are you sure you're okay here with the two new girls? They're good, but they're still green."

"I've got this," Mom assures me. "Go take care of things, but keep an open mind, Willa Elizabeth."

"Yes, ma'am," I mutter as I toss my scarf around my neck and hurry out to my—I mean Max's—car. He assured me over the phone that he'd meet me at my house, and I'm going to have to restrain myself from driving dangerously fast to get there. To see with my own two eyes that my baby is safe and whole.

I'm so fucking pissed.

Wouldn't Max know better than to take my son to the very place where his father *died?*

"What the hell is wrong with him?" I ask the car at large as I speed down the highway, praying I don't get pulled over and issued a ticket.

I don't.

I've also never made it home so fast from downtown in my life.

Max's Mercedes is in the drive, and the lights are on in the house. I put the Range Rover in park, shut it off, and without even reaching for my bag or anything else, I hurry out of the vehicle and into the house to find Alex and Max grinning from ear-to-ear, standing in my kitchen as if nothing of interest is happening.

"You." I point to Max and quickly shed my scarf and coat, tossing them onto the floor. "I'm going to need an explanation. And when I say explanation, the only appropriate answer is that someone held a mother-effing *gun* to your head and gave you no other choice but to take my son to that godforsaken deathtrap."

"Willa—"

"No. *No.*" I shake my head and stomp around the kitchen island as both of them watch me with wide eyes and somber faces. "I've made it perfectly clear to Alex how I feel about this, and you should *know* that the last place I'd want my son is on that mountain, Max."

"If you'd just listen to me—"

"Listen to what, exactly?" I stop and prop my fists on my hips. "You took it upon yourself to make a decision without even *calling me*. Max, you are *not* Alex's father, and you don't get to call these kinds of shots. These are decisions for *me* to make."

"Wills."

"No." I stop and glare at him through the tears filling my eyes. "I'm so damn angry with you. So frustrated. My heart fell to my feet when you said you took him skiing. It's a feeling I don't ever want to have again, and if you can't understand that, then I'm not sure what we're doing here. What's the point?"

"Enough," Max snaps, making me blink rapidly. "I'm happy to have a calm discussion with you about this, but I will not be yelled at and belittled by you. Especially not in front of your son, who I happen to have a lot of respect for. So, when you've calmed down, you can come find me."

He reaches for his jacket as he turns to Alex.

"I'll see you later, buddy."

"'Kay."

Alex's face is pale as he watches Max walk out the door.

"I can't believe he just left," I mutter and lean against the counter, hanging my head in frustration. I *want* to discuss this like a rational adult, but all of my worst fears flashed before my eyes at least a dozen times since I got off the phone with Max and pulled up to the house.

"Mom," Alex says softly.

"Not now, Bubba. I'm sorry, but I'm very upset."

"Mom, I need to talk to you," he says, and I can hear the urgency in his voice, so I put my own love-life issues to the side and look down at my son.

"Why are you crying?"

"Mom." He sniffles. "I'm sorry. I told Max that it would be okay if we went skiing."

Oh, God. "*Alex.*"

"I knew you would say no, and I *really* wanted to go, so I told him that it wasn't a big deal. That I was supposed to have ski lessons this year anyway, but we didn't have time for them."

"Alexander."

"I'm sorry," he whispers and brushes a tear from his cheek. "I just…my friends can ski, and I know Dad loved to ski. I wanted to go, too. And it was the *best*, Mom."

That's what I was afraid of.

"I was really good about listening and doing exactly what Max said, and he only took me on the beginner hill. It was safe the whole time, I swear."

"Alex, what you did is *so wrong.*"

"I know."

"It's not just you who got into trouble. I yelled at Max, and I was so scared."

"I know," he says again, more tears rolling down his cheeks. "I just wanted it so bad."

"You don't get to lie to get things you want, even if you want them really badly," I remind him. "I don't know what's gotten into you lately, but we are going to have a sit-down conversation."

"A serious one?"

"Probably the most serious one we've ever had. And, yes, there will be consequences."

"I know," he repeats, hanging his head. "What do we do now?"

I take a deep breath and let it out slowly, my brain whirling.

"We both need to go and apologize to Max," I decide. "Get your coat on, right now."

"Yes, ma'am."

He rushes to the mudroom for his coat, and I pick mine up off the floor, then pull the front door open and stop short when I see Max sitting on the top step, his head in his hands.

"Whoa, he's still here," Alex says, coming to a stop next to me.

"I see that," I reply. "Bubba, why don't you

go get your shower out of the way before dinner, okay? I'll be in to check on you in a few minutes."

"But, I have to—"

"And you will. In a little bit."

He nods and walks back inside. I pull the door closed behind me and sit next to Max, who hasn't even looked up, even through my conversation with Alex.

We sit in silence for about two minutes until I can't stand it anymore.

"You didn't go."

"Nope."

His hands are in fists, dangling between his knees. The sun has set, and the snow is falling. Big, heavy flakes that make the air hushed as if it holds a secret.

Because maybe it does.

It's cold enough to see my breath, but not enough to drive me inside.

"I owe you an apology," I begin, "for yelling at you without listening."

"Thank you."

"Alex admitted that he lied to you."

"He did," he agrees, then sighs. "But I'm not going to throw a kid under the bus, Wills. I'm the adult, and I made the decision to take him after he asked. He said you wouldn't mind, but I should have called."

"Yeah." I nod once. "You should have called. He's been pushing my buttons lately. When ski season started, he asked for lessons. I just can't, Max."

I sniff at the tears that want to fall.

"I get it," he replies. "But you need to remember that it wasn't the mountain that killed Cary."

"I know, but come on, Max."

"If he'd been in a car accident, would you forbid Alex from riding in cars?"

I shake my head out of frustration. He's right, I wouldn't. "I know it's not rational, but I can't change it. The thought of him being on skis absolutely terrifies me. Maybe because I see so much of his dad in him, I'm worried that he'll make a bad decision."

"You can't control that," Max says. "But now that I know you don't give your permission, I won't take him again. You have my word on that."

"I'm going to make him hate me," I whisper. "I don't want that."

"If no skiing is all it takes, well, that seems pretty silly to me. He'll be mad, but he will get over it."

I lean my head on his shoulder. It's the only physical connection between us. "I also need to apologize for being a raging bitch and throwing the whole not being his dad thing in your face."

"That stung," he admits but kisses my head.

"I'm not trying to be his dad."

"I *know*. And I'm ashamed that I said that. You didn't deserve it."

"I guess today was part of the learning curve." He kisses my hair again, then moves his arm, urging me to back up so he can wrap his arms around me and hug me close. "There are going to be moments like this because it's new territory for both of us."

"You didn't leave," I whisper.

"I couldn't go," he replies softly. "But I couldn't stay. What am I going to do with you, Wills?"

I smile. "I guess this. This was the right thing. I promise to keep the bitch reeled in."

"You're a mama bear, not a bitch," he reminds me. "Speaking of, you should go check on him."

"Will you stay? For dinner?"

"You check on him, I'll cook."

I raise my brows. "There's a lasagna in the fridge. All you have to do is pop it in the oven."

"Thank Christ."

***

"It was *so fun*," Alex says for the fortieth time this evening. Rocky is at his feet, begging for a piece of Alex's garlic bread.

Mom brought the puppy home about an hour ago while the lasagna was cooking. I think she wanted to check in and make sure I hadn't killed

Max with my bare hands.

Smart woman.

"Yes, I hear you had a lot of fun today. Which is good because you're about to lose some privileges."

"Oh, man."

"You earned it," I remind him sternly. "Now, go wash your hands and then take Rocky out one last time before bed."

"Can Max tuck me in tonight?" Alex asks, surprising me. From the look on Max's face, it surprised him, too.

"If he doesn't mind."

"Do as your mom asks, and I'll be there in a few minutes."

"Awesome." Alex runs off to the bathroom to wash his hands and brush his teeth, Rocky right on his heels. Getting the dog was the right decision. That pup is Alex's shadow and his best friend.

It's a good thing I can't take the dog away. I'm mad enough to consider it.

"C'mon, Rocky," Alex says, leading the dog to the back door. "Time to go potty."

"I need a vacation," I mutter as I set the last plate in the dishwasher.

"Where do you want to go?" Max asks, stepping to me and rubbing my shoulders from behind.

"I need to be careful what I say to you. You're

rich enough to take me anywhere."

"So? Where would you go?"

I grin and lean back into him. "Are you afraid I'm with you for your money?"

"Horrified." His voice is as dry as the desert wind. "Answer the question."

"Somewhere warm," I reply with a sigh. "I miss the sunshine. I would sit by the pool with a frosty drink and a book."

"That's it? That's your fantasy?"

"Hey, it's a damn good fantasy," I reply with a laugh. "Throw in a massage and maybe a facial, and I'd be in heaven."

"Max! I'm in bed!"

"I guess you have a job to do," I say and turn around to wrap my arms around his neck, then press my face to his throat and hold on tight, just for a minute. "Thank you."

"For what?"

"Staying."

He squeezes me tight and then lets go to walk into Alex's room. I start the dishwasher, wipe down the countertops, and then decide, *screw it,* and creep down the hall to listen to the conversation going on in my boy's room.

"I didn't mean to get anyone in trouble," Alex says quietly.

"Are you sure about that? What did you think

would happen when your mom found out where we went today?"

"I don't know," Alex replies. "I guess I didn't think about it because I was too excited."

"You have to think things through, Alex. There are always consequences, and you knew that your mom would have said no if we'd asked."

"Yeah," Alex agrees. "I'm sorry that she yelled at you."

"Well, it probably won't be the last time," Max says, making me smile.

"Really? Why would you stick around if someone is gonna yell at you all the time?"

"I didn't say it would happen all the time," Max says, a chuckle in his voice. "But from time to time, there will be arguments. That's just the way it is when you love someone. You and your mom argue, right?"

I'm stuck like stupid on "love someone."

"Yeah, we argue."

"But you still want to be around her, right?"

"Well, sure. She's my mom, and she's the best ever."

And, cue the tears. Damn these men and their sweetness!

"See? Just because we argue or yell doesn't mean we leave, Alex."

"My friend's parents used to yell at each other

all the time, and they got divorced. Are you going to get divorced?"

"We aren't married," Max reminds him. I cover my mouth, tears running unchecked over my fingers.

"It could be cool if you got married," Alex suggests. "'Cause then you'd be here all the time, not just after school. And you could come to my school on Dad Day."

"There's a Dad Day?" Max asks.

"Yeah, Grandpa usually goes with me."

Oh, my heart. How did I miss that my boy needs a father so badly? Was I just hopeful that my love would be enough for him?

"But you can't marry her if you're just gonna get divorced," Alex says as if he's thought this all through. "Because I don't think it would be good if someone else leaves."

"Who else left?" Max asks.

"Dad."

I have to walk away from the door. I can't hold the sobs back anymore, and I don't want Alex to know that his sweet words made me cry.

By the time Max comes out to the living room fifteen minutes later, I've controlled the tears and turned on the TV to the home and garden station, watching a couple trying to find the perfect mountain cabin tour homes in North Carolina.

"That took a while," I say when Max walks

into the room, looking far more exhausted than he did when he left.

"He apologized," he says as he sits next to me and takes my hand in his, kissing my knuckles. "And he's a talker."

"That he is." I laugh, remembering the few minutes that I heard. But I don't bring it up. It was a private conversation between Max and Alex. "I'm glad he apologized."

"He was worried that because we had an argument, I wouldn't want to come around anymore."

"What did you tell him?" I turn toward him and plant my elbow on the back of the couch, leaning on it and watching Max's handsome face as he thinks the past thirty minutes over.

"That it doesn't work that way. People argue, but it doesn't mean they leave."

"How many stories did he make you read?"

"No stories."

"I'm sorry, did you tuck Alexander Cary Monroe into bed?"

Max laughs and nods. "Yeah, but we had too much to talk about. It ate up all of story time."

"Sounds like it was a serious conversation."

"Pretty serious. Guy stuff," he adds, making me grin. "I could tell you, but then I'd have to kill you, and that would be unfortunate because I've grown rather fond of you."

"Well, then, we can't have that, can we?" I

lean in and kiss his cheek. "Did Alex mention that Cary's parents are coming to town next weekend?"

"He did, actually. Do they come often?"

"Every few months. They miss us. It's always good to see them."

"I think that's great."

"I'm nervous to tell them about you," I admit. "Not because I think they'll be angry or ugly about it. They're not like that. I just don't want... I don't know."

"You don't want to hurt them," Max finishes for me. "And that makes you a wonderful person, Willa Elizabeth."

"You're the second person to use my full name today."

"Who was the other?"

"My mom."

"Uh-oh, were you in trouble?"

"Maybe." I giggle, the weight of the day finally rolling off my shoulders. "Or maybe she was just making sure to drive her point home."

"Like me," he says, leaning in to kiss my forehead, then down to my nose. "You're the best there is, Willa Elizabeth."

"You can just call me Wills."

CHAPTER FOURTEEN

Willa

"THEY'RE HERE!"

Alex is jumping about the living room, Rocky on his heels, barking and dancing, sure that his master is trying to play with him.

It's chaos.

I don't hate it.

"Well, go open the door for them, silly."

I'm in the kitchen, tossing a salad and just as excited as Alex to see Jean and Dan Monroe.

"Hello, darling," Jean says, folding Alex in her ample arms, holding him close. Jean is a grandma, through and through. Gray hair, a round figure, and the happiest face on the planet. She makes you just want to curl up beside her and listen to her tell stories.

Dan walks right up to me and kisses my cheek. "How are you, sweet girl?"

"I'm great," I reply with a smile. Dan's face has more lines than it did when his son passed away, but his hair is still as dark as can be. He's a big man. Brawny. He looks like he could lift a car off the ground.

He's also the most gentle man I know.

"I need to hug my girl," Jean says, holding out her arms for me and hugging me close. "You're gorgeous as ever."

"Thank you."

"Mom, they brought presents," Alex exclaims in delight. "And it's not even my birthday anymore."

"Imagine that." I narrow my eyes on Jean, but she just smiles innocently.

"It's my job as a grandmother to spoil my grandchild." She sniffs and turns to watch Alex tear into his gifts.

"A new video game!" He rushes over to show me. "Look, it's the one I pointed out to you after Christmas."

"I see that."

"Can I play it after dinner?"

"No."

The whole room goes quiet. Alex looks down in a pout, and Jean and Dan both frown.

"Why ever not?" Jean asks.

"Alex is being punished for lying, and for manipulating a situation." Alex's cheeks turn red. "Part of that punishment is no video games for a week. So, I'll take this for now and put it with the others, and you can play it when you get your privileges back."

"Not fair," he grumbles.

"What did you say?" I ask, annoyed that he thinks he can get away with acting like this because his grandparents are here.

"Thank you," he says. He's smart enough to know when he's on my last nerve.

"Well, I think we'll hold onto the other gifts until the end of the week," Dan says sternly and steers Alex into the dining room where the table is set.

I sigh and reach for the hot pot of chili and carry it to the dining room, then return for the cornbread and salad, but Jean has already grabbed them and is following me.

"Do you want to talk about it?" she asks.

"I want to talk about a few things," I reply.

"We'll have plenty of time after dinner." She sets the food down and pats my shoulder. "It sounds like Alex coming with us for the week is happening at a good time."

I just smile and sit across from her, giving her the signal that we'll discuss it later. Alex keeps us all entertained during dinner, filling Jean and Dan in on school, his friends, and going to watch movies in Max's movie theater. Rocky lays at Alex's feet, not whining or bothering anyone through dinner.

"How did you get him to stop begging?" I ask Alex, surprised.

"I watched YouTube videos on dog training," he explains. "Before I got grounded from my electronics. Maybe you should give me my iPad back so I can keep training him."

"He'll still be trainable next week," I reply.

"But, Mom—" I cock a brow, and Alex stops arguing. He sighs deeply and rests his head in his hand. "Okay. I'll stop."

"How is the shop?" Dan asks, changing the subject.

"Busy," I reply happily. "We just had a big sale on the winter inventory, and I'm happy to report that most of it sold, giving me plenty of room for the spring stuff I have arriving next week."

"I can't believe it's almost the middle of March," Jean says, shaking her head. "I'll have to stop into the shop to see what you have left."

"I actually held a few things back for you because I knew you'd be here this week. I think you'll like them. If you don't, I can still sell them."

"You always know just what to choose for me," Jean says with a proud smile. "Thank you, dear."

"My pleasure." I specifically order pieces for Jean and my mom, and several other older ladies in the community who enjoy fashion and want higher-end options. I take pride in having something for everyone in my store, no matter their age or size.

All girls deserve to feel good in the clothes they wear.

"Is your mom still working there part-time?" Dan asks.

"Yes, she helps cover for me. I finally hired two new girls, and they're catching on quickly, so that helps, too."

"I'm so glad it's going well," Jean says as she finishes her chili, then carries her bowl to the kitchen.

"Papa, do you want to watch *Captain America* with me after dinner?" Alex asks. Evening movies or TV shows are one thing I didn't take away from him this week.

After all, I don't want to punish myself, as well.

"Of course, I do," Dan says.

After we've all finished our meals, I clear the table as Dan and Alex take Rocky outside for a quick walk.

"Talk to me," Jean says when I join her at the sink, rinsing bowls.

"I didn't think he would be so difficult at nine," I confess. "I didn't expect to suddenly have to deal with fibbing and pouting and manipulation. I was expecting it at sixteen. I'm not ready."

"Ah, the joys of parenthood," she says with a sigh. She no longer has the sadness in her eyes when she thinks of being a mom and losing her only child so suddenly. "He's a smart boy, and he knows what he wants."

"Yes, and apparently, that includes going skiing," I say and watch Jean's eyes widen. "Exactly. I've told him no over and over again this winter, but he managed to convince Max that I would be okay with it the other day, and they went."

"Oh, my," Jean says, frowning.

"I was *livid*. First at Max, and then at Alex when I learned what he pulled."

"I don't blame you," Jean says, shaking her head. "Why are you so adamant that Alex not ski?"

I stare at her a moment, shocked that she would even ask that. "What do you mean? I don't want him up there because of Cary."

Jean sighs. "I can understand that, but you can't wrap him in bubble wrap and chain him in his room. Whether it's on the ski hill or in front of your house, he could get hurt."

"Wow, I can't believe you think he should ski."

"I think you should let him do what you're comfortable with," she qualifies. "And if you're not okay with him on skis, then stick to your guns. Alex needs to learn that he will be told no in this life, and no means no."

"Yeah." I rub my forehead with my fingertips, a headache coming on. "Are you sure you're okay with taking him for the week? With the behavior stuff going on, *and* a puppy?"

"Of course," Jean says, patting my shoulder. "We've been excited to spend the week with our grandson, and the puppy will be just fine with us, too. I think you need a little break."

"That makes me feel guilty," I admit. "That I need a break from my own kid."

"It's normal," she says with a laugh. "He's wonderful, *and* a handful. Don't feel guilty. You'll be excited to see him when the week is over."

"Yes, I will." I take another deep breath and prepare myself for the next part of the conversation. "I have something else to tell you."

"Go ahead."

"I've been dating Max." I say it in a rush, wanting to get it out as fast as possible, and cringe as I wait for her response.

"Oh, that? I know." She grins and pats my hand.

"You know?"

"He was here for Alex's party, Alex talks about him all the time, and I do have conversations with your mother, Willa."

I blink at her, surprised because she looks perfectly calm. "And you don't mind?"

"Why on earth would I mind?" She frowns, then gives me a look as if a light bulb illuminates over her head. "Did you think this would be a thing?"

"Maybe."

"Willa, it's been *nine years*. Neither Dan nor I expect you to live as a nun. You're young and beautiful and wonderful. You deserve to move on. You need to move on."

Tears threaten. I feel relief and happiness and still so much love from Jean.

"You're both so wonderful to me."

"You're like a daughter to us, and that'll never change. Do you remember not long before you married Cary and I asked you what would happen if Max came back to town?"

"Of course. I told you that it wouldn't matter. I loved Cary."

"I believed you. I still believe you. I hope that isn't one of the reasons you were nervous to tell me about this exciting new time in your life."

I bite my lip.

"Darling, life goes on. It took a while for Dan and me to heal, but we have. And so have you. It's time for you to truly *live* your life, not just for your son, but for yourself, too. Cary would want that. And I've always liked Max."

I laugh and wipe a tear from my cheek. "Me, too."

"I just hope that if this turns into something permanent, Dan and I still have a place here."

"Oh, Jean." I reach for her and wrap my arms tightly around her. "Always. You are an important part of our family. We love you and Dan so much."

"Well, then," she says, sniffling at tears of her own, "that's settled."

***

"Okay, he has enough clothes for a month, but you can always call me if you need more."

"We have a washer and dryer," Dan reminds me with a smile. They never sold their home in Cunningham Falls. Instead, they rent it out as a vacation rental when they're not in town, and live in it when they are. It's worked out wonderfully for them. "And you're across town."

Jeans sends Dan a look, but before I can ask what it means, Alex hugs me around the waist fiercely.

"Have a good week, Mom," he says. "Don't worry about a thing."

I squat next to him and brush his hair off his forehead. I'll need to take him for a haircut next week. "Remember what we talked about, Bubba. I need you to be on your very best behavior."

"I will," he says. "I promise. You don't have to worry."

"I'll call every evening before you go to bed to check in, and if you need anything at all, just have Nana or Papa call me, okay?"

"Yep," he says with a nod. "Love you, Mom."

Then he's off with Rocky, running into the house he knows as a second home.

"Thanks again," I say. "Please call if he gets to be too much."

"Pfft," Jean says. "He can't dish out anything

we can't handle. Now you go and rest a bit."

"Okay." I hug them both. "See you soon. I'll call tonight."

They wave me off, and I climb into Max's car and pull away from their house, headed to yoga.

I quickly call Tom at the garage to check on my car. This is just getting ridiculous.

"Hey, Willa," he says, far too cheerfully. I'm about to get bad news.

"It's not ready," I guess.

"Can't say that it is," he confirms. "They sent us the wrong parts again, so I have a call in for the right ones."

"Tom, should I just have it towed somewhere else? If you're too busy for it, just say so."

"Nah, Willa. I'm sorry it's been a huge fiasco. I'm going to fix it for just the cost of the parts. I won't charge you for labor. Give me one more week to resolve it, okay?"

I sigh. "Okay. But, seriously, just be honest if it's not something you can do."

"Deal," he says, then talks to someone in his shop. "Oops, better go, Willa. I'll be in touch."

He hangs up, and I shake my head. I've grown used to the Rover. I actually *love* it, but I'll never admit that to Max. Knowing him, he'd sign the title over to me.

He's generous and sweet. But I don't need his car. I already feel bad that I've had it as long as I have. It did turn out to be helpful, though. A car rental would have been expensive, and my mom couldn't have been without her vehicle this long.

I'll have to do something extra nice to thank Max for loaning it to me.

I pull into a space in front of the yoga studio, pull my mat out of the backseat, and walk inside. I'm a little early, so only Fallon is here.

"Hi, Willa," she says with a welcoming smile. Fallon is petite and slender and strong from all of the yoga, with long, dark hair and brown eyes. She has a tiny, dark mole next to her eye that makes her look exotic.

"Good morning," I reply and spread out my mat in my usual spot at the back of the class, then walk up to join her. "How are you?"

"I actually overslept this morning for the first time in a very long time," she admits.

"You must have needed the sleep."

"I suppose so," she says with a shrug. "I scored some really great deals at your sale this week."

"Oh, I'm so glad. What did you pick up?"

She tells me about her new tops and shoes, and just when she's finished, Jenna walks in.

"I overslept," Jenna says in a rush.

"So did I," Fallon says with a frown. "I wonder what phase the moon is in?"

"Whatever it is, it's making me sleep," Jenna says with a yawn, then smiles at me. "But I made it."

"Good. You look really cute for just rolling out of bed."

"Christian tried to keep me there, but I wasn't about to miss yoga with my bestie," she says, smiling smugly.

"Wow, I'm proud of you," I reply. A couple of other women arrive, but the group is small today. "I wonder if everyone is sleeping in?"

"Could be," Jenna says, then shoots me a weird smile like she has a secret.

"What's up with you?" I ask as we stand on our mats.

"Nothing." She scoffs. That's a clear sign she's telling me a fib.

"I don't buy it."

"There is literally *nothing* going on," she says, stretching her arms above her head. "What's going on with you?"

I narrow my eyes at her. "Why does your voice sound like that?"

"Like what?"

"Like Mickey Mouse?"

She shrugs. "Maybe I'm coming down with something."

I watch her for a moment more, then turn my attention to Fallon. We're quiet today as we move from pose to pose, breathing and centering. One of the things I love most about Fallon's class is that she incorporates guided meditation, which makes me feel completely grounded by the time class is over.

"*Namaste*, friends," Fallon says as we finish up.

"*Namaste*," we reply in unison.

"You know what would feel good?" Jenna asks. "Sunshine. We haven't seen sunshine in forever."

"Have your rich fiancé take you somewhere sunny," I suggest, but she just smiles that strange smile. "Okay, you're acting really weird today."

"Gotta go," she says, kissing my cheek then waving as she jogs off to her car.

Is she pregnant? Morning drinking?

I shake my head, climb into the Rover, and drive toward home. I love that the sale is over, and the shop has slowed down a bit. With my two new employees, Brittney and Melanie, catching on so quickly, I can go home, take a leisurely shower, and roll into work whenever I like.

God bless my mom for recommending that I hire both of them.

I frown when I see Max's car parked in front of my house but then get a little excited. I have plenty of time to squeeze in some sexy time before work today.

I climb out of the car as he joins me and pulls me in for a long, deep kiss.

"Well, good morning to you, too," I murmur when he pulls back.

"I have a surprise for you," he says.

"What's that?"

"We're going on vacation."

I blink, staring at him, sure I've heard him wrong. "What?"

"Vacation," he repeats. "I've packed you a bag, and the plane is ready to go."

"You packed for me?"

"What you'll need, yes. Come on, trust me."

"I need to call Jean and let her know. And my mom, ask her to cover for me at the shop—"

"All done," he replies with a smile. "Jean knows where we'll be and how to reach us at all times. And your mom is filling in for you at the shop. It's all set."

"I need a shower."

"You have thirty minutes." He kisses me again, softer this time. "I need some time alone with you. In the sunshine."

In the sunshine.

That's why Jenna was being weird! She knew.

"Do I get to know where we're going?"

"When we get there, yes," he says and plants a quick kiss on my lips then smacks my ass. "Now, get in the shower so we can get this show on the road."

"Are we really going in your private plane?"

"It's the only way to fly."

CHAPTER FIFTEEN

Willa

I'M ONE HUNDRED PERCENT sure I've found heaven.

It's located just south of San Diego at a resort nestled on the cliffs above the ocean. I'm sitting poolside with a Coke, extra ice, at my elbow and a book in my hand. Of course, I'm under the shade of an umbrella because I haven't seen the sun in several months and I don't want to burn.

The Pacific Ocean is spread out before me in deep blue splendor. The wind is minimal, so the waves are mild and soothing.

I haven't seen any whales yet, but I'm keeping an eye out.

My phone vibrates with a text.

Jenna: So, did you make it down there safely?

I smirk, set my book aside, and settle in to chat with my best friend.

Me: Yes. You totally knew! That's why you were acting weird this morning.

The three dots wink at me as she types a reply, so I take a sip of my Coke and glance at Max, who's sitting next to me, sans umbrella, absorbed in whatever is happening on his laptop.

Apparently, this is vacation for *me*, but while I rest, he's working.

I have a feeling work is relaxing for Max, though.

Jenna: Of course, I knew! And I can't keep secrets from you. I shouldn't have gone to yoga.

I laugh.

Me: You are a horrible liar! But it was a fantastic surprise. Hold on, I'll take a photo of what I'm doing right now.

I snap a photo of my toes with the pool and ocean beyond in the frame and send it to her.

Jenna: I hate you. That looks AMAZING!

Me: It is. So warm! I had no idea that Max owns a condo down here.

"You okay?" Max asks me.

"Oh, yeah, I'm just texting with Jenna." I tell him all about yoga this morning, and he laughs. "She's not good at keeping secrets from me. We never have to. We tell each other everything."

"I'll remember that in the future," he says with a grin. "Are you enjoying yourself?"

"Are you kidding? No one is asking me for anything. I don't have to pick anyone up, drop them off, fix them dinner, or clean up puppy accidents. I may never want to leave."

His lips twitch. "You love those things."

"I do," I admit as my phone buzzes with another text from Jenna. "And I'll love them when I get home. In the meantime, I'm going to enjoy the break."

"Excellent," he replies. "I'm going for a swim."

"Enjoy."

He leans over and kisses me before peeling his shirt over his head and diving into the deep end of the pool.

Holy shit. Max without a shirt on is something to write home about. He's tanned and firm.

Firm. Muscles for days. Abs that would make a Greek god weep with joy. And the V at his hips?

Ridiculous. Just ridiculous. Max does things to my lady parts that haven't even been invented yet. How does he do it?

Sexy powers, that's what he has.

I lick my lips and pick up the phone.

Jenna: Max owns property all over. We should use his place in NYC sometime and go shopping! We could call it a business trip for you.

Me: That's not a bad idea at all! We will do that.

Jenna: Okay, go have fun. Enjoy the sun! I don't want to know about the rest. ;)

I set the phone aside, take another sip of my Coke, then pick up the book I've been reading by Jennifer Probst. I don't get to read often, but when I do, romance is my go-to.

But the warm, fresh air is soothing, and the sound of the water makes my eyes heavy. So, before long, I set my book aside and just lazily watch Max swim his laps and the ocean waves beyond. I don't remember the last time I felt this pampered, this relaxed.

This treasured.

I admit, Max did good. He listened when I said I needed a break, and he gave me exactly what I dreamed of: sunshine, a book, and a frosty beverage.

I wonder if we'd be in the Maldives if that's where I said I wanted to go.

Probably.

I also wonder if women have taken advantage of Max in the past. Or tried, anyway. I'm sure they have, although I really don't want to think about Max with other women. I mean, I know he wasn't a recluse when he left town all those years ago. There have been other women.

Ew.

I just don't want to think about it.

I shove the thought aside and settle in to doze

and enjoy the view.

I never fall asleep, and a short time later, Max comes walking out of the pool. Thank the good Lord I'm awake to see that magnificence.

The water sluices down his toned body, making my mouth water. I wonder if I can convince him to go back to his condo with me so we can get naked. It is vacation, after all.

"You look—"

"Lazy?" I ask with a grin. "Spoiled rotten?"

"If this is your definition of spoiled, we have more work to do," he says, shaking his head.

"I know this is probably small potatoes for you, but it's a big deal for me," I remind him. "How long have you owned this place?"

"The resort, or the condo?" he asks with a sly grin.

"You own the *whole resort*?" I squeak, sitting up in surprise. "Jesus Christ, Max."

"I bought the condo about four years ago. I wanted a little getaway that wasn't too far from Montana but was warm in the winter."

"This fits that bill."

"I liked the all-inclusive style of this place. There are six restaurants on the property, along with a spa, and charter services for fishing. All kinds of stuff. And half of the property, where my condo is, is privately-owned, while the other side has nightly rentals."

"Smart," I say, nodding. "Very smart. This would be a beautiful spot for weddings or reunions. Honeymoons. And I bet those who don't want or can't afford to buy a condo but want luxury love coming here."

"Exactly," he says. "It's a notch above a Super 8."

"A notch or two," I say with a laugh. "Now, tell me about owning the whole place."

He shrugs a shoulder as if it's no big thing.

"It discreetly came up for sale about two years ago. The owners were headed to bankruptcy. I didn't want it to be sold off and changed. I think this place is special."

"Were they headed for bankruptcy because of personal reasons, or because the resort was sinking them?"

He tilts his head. "I'm a shrewd businessman, Willa. The resort is turning a nice profit annually. The previous owners mismanaged their money."

"I never doubted you," I say and stretch my arms high above my head. "From what I've seen of it in the couple of hours we've been here, I love it."

"I'll show you more," he promises as he checks the time. "I wanted to get you out to the pool ASAP. But now, we have to go because you have an appointment."

"I do?" I frown and sip the last of my Coke. "With whom? Are you going to make me sit with your in-house real estate agents and listen to a spiel about becoming an owner in exchange for my stay here?"

He laughs and shakes his head. "No, smartass. I have you set up for a few hours in the spa."

I feel my eyes widen in surprise as I stand next to him. Before he can tug his shirt over his head, I launch myself into his arms and kiss him hard.

"You're the best," I say, brushing my fingers through his hair. "And not just because of all of this. You're so damn thoughtful and *good*, Max."

"Don't say that too loud. I don't want the employees to hear you." He grins and drags his fingertips down my cheek. "You deserve all of this and much more, Wills. But for today, it's going to be lazy pool sitting and pampering at the spa."

"Thank you."

I take his offered hand, and he leads me into the main building, up one flight of the grand staircase, and to the end of a hallway where water falls on either side of wide, glass doors.

Grandview Spa.

"You'll see why it's called that in a minute," he says with a wink, then opens the door for me and leads me through a lobby with another water feature and shelves full of skincare for sale. "When you're finished, you're welcome to shop through here and take anything you like. Just let Sarah know."

"Hi," a redhead with thick, black-rimmed glasses behind the counter says with a smile. "I'm

Sarah. You must be Willa."

"Nice to meet you," I reply. Sarah doesn't stare dreamy-eyed at Max. She's completely professional and kind as she asks me to disclose any medical concerns.

"This is where I bow out," Max says, pulling me in for a hug. "Enjoy yourself. Take all the time you want. The only thing not on the menu for you today is massage."

I frown. "Why?"

"Don't ask questions." He kisses my forehead, then turns to Sarah. "She can have anything we offer. Just write it down, and I'll settle up later. That includes the items in the store."

"Of course, Mr. Hull," Sarah says with a polite smile. "If you'll follow me, we'll get you a locker and ready to go."

"See you later," Max says, then kisses me softly again and walks out.

"Okay, it sounds like I'm all yours," I say with a grin. "It's been a while since I've been to the spa."

"I'm excited for you," Sarah says. "I have a robe for you, along with slippers. Go ahead and stow your things in the locker. You can sit in here." She leads me into a room that feels like it's sitting *over* the ocean.

"Wow."

"Best view in the resort," she says with a nod. "So, if you'd like thirty minutes or so in here before we start your treatment, we can accommodate that."

"Do you have tea?"

"Of course."

"I'd love that."

Sarah shows me a menu of services, and I choose a ninety-minute hydration facial and a mani/pedi, then change into my robe and sit in a deep, soft chair facing the water.

Sarah brings me some tea, and for the next thirty minutes, I watch boats float by, surfers try to catch some small waves, and am alone in the quiet with my thoughts.

Other women come and go, sitting for a few minutes before or after their treatments.

It's a calming, serene space that smells of lavender.

I could live here.

"Willa?"

I turn with a smile. "That's me."

"I'm Tia. I'll be giving you your facial," she says. She's a tiny Asian woman with beautiful skin and perfect makeup.

"Thank you. Tia, you might be my favorite person today."

"I hear that a lot."

***

I've been buffed and polished and pampered silly.

After my facial, Sarah delivered an amazing late lunch of Caesar salad with smoked salmon and chocolate cheesecake for dessert.

I don't know what I did in this life to deserve all of this goodness, but I hope I keep doing it.

Not to mention, Max is going to get the blow-job of his life tonight.

I giggle as I ride the elevator up to Max's condo, still wearing the robe Sarah gave me earlier. I decided to keep it.

When I say *condo*, the word doesn't do the place justice. Max's space is the penthouse, spanning a *ton* of square footage. It feels way bigger than my house. There's also a gorgeous outdoor living space with views of the ocean that I plan to spend some time in tomorrow.

This week is going to be all about lying about in different comfortable spots with lots of delicious food.

The doors open directly into Max's space, and I frown, wondering if I came to the right place. I put in the code Max gave me this morning, but the condo is...different.

Flameless candles flicker on either side of the foyer. Huge flower arrangements sit between them, on the tables, and down the hallway that leads to the open-concept kitchen and living areas.

The gas fireplace is lit, and red rose petals are sprinkled on the floor.

And Max is standing next to a massage table

set up near the floor-to-ceiling windows.

"How was your afternoon?" he asks softly.

"Amazing." I swallow hard. "What's this?"

"A pony," he says dryly, making me laugh. "This is why the massage wasn't an option for you downstairs." He holds out his hand for mine, then pulls me to him. He drags his fingertips down my cheek. "Your skin is so soft."

"Tia gives the best facials in all fifty states," I inform him. "Who's giving me the massage?"

"Oh, you think the massage is for *you*?" he asks and kisses my cheek.

"You're funny today." I run my fingers through the soft hair at the back of his neck. "How was *your* afternoon?"

"Good. I got some work done, and had this set up for when you got back."

"It's really pretty."

"You've hardly looked at it."

"You're also really pretty," I inform him. "And I'm grateful."

With his eyes still pinned to mine, he slips his finger under the belt holding my robe closed.

"I see you like the robes."

"I'm keeping this one."

He tugs the knot free, and the robe falls open, exposing my naked body beneath.

"You're dressed perfectly for a massage."

I cock a brow. "Or, you know, other things."

His lips twitch in that way they do as he pushes the robe over my shoulders, letting it pool around my feet.

"Why don't you get on the table?" he asks quietly, kissing my nose. "And I'll give you a massage while you watch the sunset."

I look outside and gasp. I was so wrapped up in Max and how he makes me feel that I didn't even notice the riot of orange and purple in the sky over the water.

"That's gorgeous."

"It pales in comparison to you," he replies as he peels back the sheet and blanket, gesturing for me to lie down.

How can I refuse that?

I can't.

So, I get cozy on the crisp, comfortable sheets, and rather than put my face in the cradle, I turn to the side so I can actually watch the sunset before me.

"This ranks up there as one of the best days ever," I say as his hands run down my back on either side of my spine, then back up again, making me sigh happily.

"I'm glad," he says. "Now, don't judge me too harshly. I'm no professional."

"This is *so good*." I sigh as he digs into the area next to my shoulder blade.

"You have the softest skin," he murmurs. "And a little freckle right here."

"I don't have freckles." I can't help but close my eyes and just enjoy what he's doing to my body. That low hum of arousal is there as it always is when Max is within a mile of me, but I'm also so relaxed, hovering in that space between being fully awake and asleep.

It's a good place to be.

"You have one," he repeats, then covers my back with the blanket and moves down to my leg. He pays attention to my calf, then moves up to my thigh. To my surprise, he keeps going until his fingertips skim over the lips of my pussy, sending me from pleasantly relaxed to *highly* aroused instantly.

"You like that," he says.

"Of course, I like that." I take a deep breath, and he does it again, making me bite my lip. But then he moves back down my leg before moving over to the next one. The calf receives plenty of attention, then the thigh, before his fingers wreak havoc on my core once again, making me moan in pleasure.

"Max."

"Time to turn over."

But rather than lie on my back, I sit on the side of the table and pull him between my legs, my fingers running beneath the band of his shorts and skimming over the head of his hard dick.

"I've had a lot of pampering today," I say, enjoying the way he's breathing hard, his eyes hot with lust. "And it was awesome. But now, I want to pamper you."

"Taking care of you is all I need."

I lean in and press a kiss to his collarbone. "You're sweet." I kiss his chest. "And I appreciate you." I kiss his nipple over his shirt, then slip my hands under the hemline and over his smooth, warm skin. "But it's my turn."

I slowly peel his clothes off him, my fingers skimming over his flesh.

"Now what?" he asks.

"Let's switch positions. You lie on the table."

He cocks a brow but doesn't argue as I hop off and gesture for him to lie down, on his back. I splash some massage oil in my hands and take my time rubbing his thighs, up his sides, and across his shoulders before trailing my fingertips down to the rigid cock lying heavily on his belly.

As soon as I cup him in my hands, he hisses in a breath through his teeth, making me feel powerful. I play with him for a moment, jerking him softly, then firmly. Slow, then fast.

Finally, I lean over and lick him from the root to the tip, and he jackknifes off the table.

"Jesus, Wills."

"You like that?" I don't expect an answer as I take him into my mouth and suck gently, then push down until the tip tickles the back of my throat before firming my lips and pulling back up.

"You keep that up, and I'll come in your mouth."

"I'm doing it right, then."

I repeat the motion, over and over again while still massaging the shaft and his balls, until he grips onto my hair and loses himself completely.

I swallow, then kiss his hip and his lower abdomen as he catches his breath.

"Whoa," he says at last, making me laugh.

"I've been saying that all day."

CHAPTER SIXTEEN

Max

"I DON'T KNOW THAT I'm ready to go home," Willa says with a wistful sigh, leaning her forehead against the window of the plane as we take off from the airport.

"We can go back anytime you want," I remind her and reach over to take her hand in mine. The past week was what we both needed: time to reconnect without interruptions. To just *be* together. She ended up borrowing a laptop so she could peruse her favorite suppliers for her store, which didn't bother me in the least because I also spent time working.

But we also had plenty of time to talk, about everything from the weather to our deepest dreams and wishes. To make love and cuddle while we watched the whales breaching in the ocean.

To be us.

But we both miss Alex, and it's time to get back to real life in Montana.

"If you don't want to go to San Diego," I continue, "we can go anywhere else you like, and take Alex with us. The plane is always available."

"Thank you," she says, then squirms in her seat. "You do know that I'm not using you for the money, right?"

I narrow my eyes at her. "This is a thing for you. You've mentioned it several times."

"I just know that women must throw themselves at you and take advantage of what you can buy them. I'm not like that."

I clear my throat. "Let's take care of this subject right here and now so we don't have to revisit it again. I hate that the money makes you uncomfortable, Wills. You once loved me when I didn't have two nickels to rub together."

"The money doesn't matter to me," she clarifies. "That's what I'm trying to say. I'd be with you whether you have it or not."

"I appreciate that," I reply and squeeze her hand. "But I *do* have it. A lot of it, like I told you before."

"I know."

"And I can give you your heart's desire, any day of the week. I don't say that to sound arrogant or like an ass. It just is. I don't think you're here because of that. Hell, it took us *years* to get here, Wills. So, no, I don't think it's because of the money."

"I'm glad." She nods once, then boosts herself into my lap, straddling me. "It's all about your body."

"Really?" My eyebrows climb into my hairline as my hands find the nice, round globes of her tight ass. "Well, that's convenient. I guess the dad bod is definitely out. I'd better keep working out."

"I don't want to sound shallow or anything," she says while unbuttoning my jeans, "but, yeah. Work out."

She yanks the jeans open and traces a finger down the sides of my hips.

"It's this. This is what makes me wetter than I can say."

"Is that so?"

"You have sexy powers," she continues, making me snort. "No, really. Screw the money; it's this body and your hands and the way you smirk at me."

She's in a blue sundress with a denim jacket that she brought along for when we reach Montana. It won't be warm enough, but now I'm eternally grateful for the easy access as my hands slide under the dress to find her ass *naked.*

"You're not wearing anything under there."

"I'm wearing a bra," she says. "Because you know, mom boobs."

"Hey, I like your boobs." I dip my head to kiss

one, just out of principle. "Don't dis your tits."

She's grinding against me, sending me into crazy town, which seems to be easy for her. All she has to do is *look* at me, and I'm hard as a rock.

It seems some things never change.

Finally, she slips over me, taking me inside her, and begins to ride me like a woman possessed.

"You feel so damn good," she groans, her fingers in my hair. "Who knew plane sex could be so fun?"

"Not me," I reply and hold onto her hips, guiding her. "But we're going to do this more often, I'll tell you that right now."

"Oh, good." She tips her head back, a sure sign that her orgasm is close. "Jesus, Max, I'm gonna come already."

I reach back and tickle her anus, which is something new I learned this week that drives her wild. She gasps and spasms around me, milking me with an intense orgasm, and just as she starts to come out the other side, I follow her, pushing up and grinding my pubic bone against her clit.

Once I've caught my breath, I set her on the seat next to me and walk back to the restroom to get a wet cloth and a dry towel to clean us up.

"That was fun," she says with a wicked grin after I dispose of the towels.

"Agreed."

"I love you, Max."

My gaze whips to hers, surprised and elated to hear the words.

"I know it's not a super romantic time to say it, but I do. And I'm grateful for every minute with you, at home and anywhere else."

I scoop her up again, cradling her to me, and kiss the fuck out of her.

"I love you, too, Wills." I tip my forehead against hers. "I never stopped loving you, all these years."

She blinks slowly, soaking it in.

"Same here." She sighs. "I felt guilty about that for a long time."

"You carry around too much guilt."

She nods. "I do, you're right. I guess I worry about hurting others, and if I'd admitted before that I still loved you, it would have hurt Cary, his parents, and me. Because you weren't mine anymore."

"I'm yours now." I kiss her cheek, her jaw, and then her lips. "I'm *always* going to be yours."

She grins and snuggles against me. "Oh, good, because if there was a blond bimbo, I'd have to kill her, and I look horrible in orange."

"Not to mention, you can't get spa treatments in prison."

"And that would be awful." She giggles. "I miss Alex. It sounded like he was having a good time with Jean and Dan. Jean said he's been good for her, and he did his homework without an issue."

"Good." She nestles herself under my chin. "I'm sorry he's been difficult lately."

"I think it's a phase," she replies softly. "It'll pass. Maybe he's having a tough time adjusting to having a guy around. He loves you, and is always excited to see you, but it's an adjustment all the same."

"True." I nod, thinking it over. "Do you want me to have a talk with him?"

"If the moment is right, and you want to talk to him, it won't bother me," she says. "Oh, and I spoke with Tom right before we went to California. I forgot to tell you in all the excitement. He still doesn't have an ETA on my car."

You have a car. But I don't say it. She can keep the Rover. I know she likes it; she just won't ask for it. Which is another thing I love about her.

"Like I said, there's no rush on that."

She nods. "Thanks."

"You don't have to thank me." I kiss her hair. "Do you want to nap a bit before we land?"

"Can I stay in your lap?"

"Of course."

"Then, yes. I want to nap."

***

"Hi, Jean, how are things?" Willa asks from the car on the way to her house. "We did land, and are on the way to my house now. We should be there in about ten minutes or so. Do you want to bring

Alex to the house, or should I come and get him? …That would be awesome, thank you. …What do you mean?"

I glance at her as her voice changes to concern. She looks at me with wide, brown eyes.

"How long has he been throwing up? Oh, gosh, Jean. I'm so sorry. …Okay, see you then."

"What's up?"

"Alex has the flu." She rubs her fingers over her forehead. "I wish she'd told me. He's been throwing up for twenty-four hours."

"Do we need to go get him?"

"No, they're bringing him home."

"He's going to be okay," I remind her.

"I know. I just hate it when he's sick. I'm always with him." She sighs. "Oh, well, it'll be fine."

I pull into her driveway and quickly unpack the car. Shortly after, Jean and Dan arrive.

"Mom," Alex says with tears in his eyes when they come inside. "I threw up in the car."

"Oh, no." Willa cringes. "I'm so sorry."

"It'll clean up," Jean says. "He got most of it in the bucket."

"I can clean it up now," I offer, but Dan shakes his head.

"It really isn't that bad," Dan says, reaching out to shake my hand. "How are you, Max?"

"I'm well, thank you."

"I'm so glad you had a nice time," Jean says with a smile.

"I'm just sorry that Alex got sick."

Rocky sniffs about as if he hasn't been here in a month, then he walks into his kennel and lays down.

Alex has trained him well already.

"We're going to get out of the way," Jean says. "We'll be in town another week, so if you need anything at all, you just call."

"Thanks so much," Willa says, leading Alex down the hall to his bedroom. "I'll call you later."

I see the couple out, then join Willa and Alex. She's just pulling fresh pajamas over the little boy's head.

"You can rest in your own bed," she says before pulling him in for a hug. "You know the drill. Get comfy, and I'll go fetch you a puke bowl, a towel, and some crackers."

"'Kay," he says. "Can I have Rocky?"

"I'll bring him back with me," she promises and gestures for me to follow her to the kitchen. "This isn't how I imagined saying this, but thanks for this week. I had a great time."

"It sounds like you're kicking me out."

She laughs humorlessly. "You definitely don't have to stay. The next day or so isn't going to be enjoyable or sexy. Let me get him back on his feet, and then I'll call you."

Without answering, I lean in and kiss her forehead. "I'll see you in a bit."

But her mind is already occupied as she searches for a big bowl and the other supplies for Alex. I leave, calling my mom as I pull out of the driveway.

"Hey, bud," she says. "How are you?"

"I'm great," I reply. "But Alex has the flu. Willa's with him, and I thought I'd go to the store for supplies. I just don't know what those are. I need mom help."

Her voice is full of joy when she says, "I love this phone call. Okay, he's going to need some Gatorade. He'll get dehydrated fast, so keep offering him lots of fluids. Crackers will be easy on his tummy. Maybe some Jell-O or pudding. Bland things that don't upset his stomach more are the key.

"I'd start there. He'll also get bored as he starts to feel better, so plan to watch a lot of TV."

"I can do that," I reply. "Okay, this is a good start. Thanks."

"Watch his fever. If it stays high, take him to the doctor. Oh, and you'll need children's Tylenol for the fever."

"Jesus, just text me a list."

She laughs in my ear. "How's Willa?"

"She's great. Worried now, of course."

"And how are things between the two of you?"

I should have known this would turn into a

Q&A session.

"Good."

"Come on, Max, give me more than that. Are you serious?"

"Oh, yeah. I'm gonna marry her for sure."

"Don't play with my emotions."

"I'm not."

There's a moment of silence, and then Mom lets out a loud whoop.

"It's about damn time!"

"I take it you approve?"

"Yes, and I'll gain a grandson. I couldn't be more excited. I'll let you go; I know it's going to be a busy couple of days with Alex being sick."

"Love you, Mom."

"Love you, too." I can hear her move the phone away from her face, but she doesn't hang up before I hear her yell, "We have to go to Montana!"

I hurry through the store, checking the list Mom texted over shortly after our talk. I add some wine for Willa, along with some snacks for her and me, and a frozen pizza for dinner, then hurry back to her place.

I walk in to chaos.

There's crying and dog whines coming from Alex's room, so I leave the bags of groceries on the kitchen island and hurry back.

Alex is covered in vomit, as is Willa, and Rocky

is on the floor at the foot of the bed, watching it all unfold.

We're all just lucky the puppy isn't leaping in to eat what's covering the two people I love.

"Okay," I say, surprising both of them. I take Willa's shoulders in my hands and kiss her forehead. "You go take a shower. I got this."

"What are you doing here?" Her eyes already look tired. "It's really okay if you go home."

"Haven't you figured it out yet?" I ask, shaking my head. "We're in this together. I went to the store and bought provisions, which are currently on the kitchen island. You go get a shower and put those away. I'm going to get Alex fixed up."

She stares at me wordlessly, then blinks rapidly and kisses my cheek, careful not to press herself against me.

"Thank you. I'll be ten minutes."

She hurries off, and I turn to Alex, who's sniffling.

"Let's go to the bathroom and get you cleaned up, buddy."

"Okay." He doesn't argue as I help him strip out of the pajamas that were clean thirty minutes ago and into the shower.

"Are you okay here while I change your bedsheets?"

"Yeah. I don't want to wash my hair."

"No yuckies in your hair, so I think you're

safe." I kiss his cheek and hurry back to his room, where I strip the bed, put the linens in the laundry, and find clean ones in a hall closet.

Just as I finish making the bed, Rocky hops onto it and turns a circle, settling in to rest.

"Good boy," I say, petting his head and scratching his ears. "You stay here and get ready to snuggle your human. I'll have him back here in a flash."

I find another set of clean PJs and rush back to the bathroom.

"How's it going in there?" I ask.

"I feel a little better," Alex says, his voice weak.

"Good. Are you all rinsed off?"

"Yeah."

"You can get out then. There are clean clothes by the sink. Are you okay by yourself?"

"Yes, sir."

I grin. Even when Alex doesn't feel well, he has his manners. He may be pushing his mom's patience lately, but Willa's still doing something right.

"I'll meet you back in your bedroom."

I walk out to the kitchen to find a fresh Willa unpacking grocery bags.

"This is incredible," she says with tears in her voice.

"It's just Gatorade and pizza," I say, not sure how to navigate this.

"No, it's not." She shakes her head. "It's a lot more than that. I don't remember the last time I had someone here to help. My mom's awesome, but it's—"

"It's not the same." I tug her to me and rub my hands up and down her back soothingly. "It's not the same as having a partner."

"No." She sniffles and looks up at me. "I'm afraid to get too used to this, Max. To depend on it. I'm too accustomed to being a one-woman show, and I'm *good* at it. I don't know what I'd do if I had to go back to that once I settle into *this*."

"Just trust me," I reply and kiss her forehead. "And don't overthink it. I'm just here to help with the flu today, Wills. And I love you, so I'm not going to leave you here to fend for yourself. That would just be cruel."

"Well, I guess there's no time like the present to jump into the deep end. You've seen him when he's fun and playful, and even when he's being a handful. Now, you get the rough stuff. We'll see if you're still here in two days."

"Is that a challenge?"

"It's a fact."

"Have the others before always bailed when it got rough?"

She sighs. "I've never given them the opportunity to make it this far. This is new territory for both of us."

I can hear Alex emerge from the bathroom, so I

quickly tug her to me and kiss her hard.

"I'll be here. In two days. In twenty years. And I'll prove it to you, one day at a time."

CHAPTER SEVENTEEN

Willa

"I'M SO BORED," Alex whines, a peanut butter and jelly sandwich in one hand, and the remote control to the TV in the other.

It's Sunday evening, and his fever finally broke this afternoon. Which means, he's feeling much better. He moved from his bedroom to the living room this morning, where he's watched everything from *Captain America*—for the twentieth time—to *Harry Potter*. Rocky has been great about sticking close to his boy for cuddles and food scraps.

They're a team now.

"I know, Bubba, but you have to rest. You're still getting better," I remind him.

"At least I get to go to school tomorrow," he murmurs as I walk into the kitchen.

Max walks in from outside, shaking snow from his jacket and boots.

"We got another foot, easy," he says with a grin. He's been here since we got home two days ago, helping with everything from cool baths to bring the fever down to taking Rocky outside to go potty.

The billionaire who made *People*'s sexiest people in the world list has become quite domesticated.

"Thanks for shoveling," I reply and boost myself up on my toes to plant a kiss on his cheek. "Want a peanut butter and jelly sandwich?"

"Is that even a question? Of course, I do." He pats my butt as he walks past me to wash his hands in the kitchen sink. "How's the patient?"

"Bored," I reply with a sigh. "But feeling better."

"My mom said this would be a stage of the process," he says, drying his hands on a towel.

"You talked to your mom?" I ask with a grin.

"Of course. I didn't know what to get at the store, so I called her."

"How is she?"

He leans in and presses his lips to my ear, sending a shiver down my back. "She's elated that I'm with you."

That makes me feel warm and happy. I always loved Max's parents.

"Well, that's good."

He kisses my cheek. "It's not bad. Does he need anything?"

"He says he's excited to go back to school tomorrow, but I'm not sure about sending him."

Max nods but doesn't say anything.

"What do you think?"

"I'm not a parent," he reminds me, and I immediately feel like shit again for telling him that he's not Alex's dad last week.

"You're an adult who cares about my kid, and I'm asking for your opinion. Please."

"Well, he hasn't been fever-free for twenty-four hours yet, so he could still infect someone else at school. Not to mention, he needs to rest, continue with the fluids, and we need to get more food into him."

"How do you know this?"

"I consulted WebMD," he says, his voice full of pride, which makes me smile. He truly does love my boy. "Besides, I really would rather he was here where we can keep an eye on him. What if he relapses? And you know the teacher won't look out for him the way we will."

"I understand." I slip my hand into his and link our fingers. "You're quite protective, you know."

"I protect what's mine," he says softly but doesn't elaborate. "So, I say he stays home one more day."

"I agree." I nod and walk into the living room with another bottle of Gatorade and a sleeve of saltines. "Bubba, I think it's best if you stay home one more day."

"Oh, man," he says in disappointment. "Am I being punished? I didn't get sick on purpose."

"No, you're not." I feel his forehead, then lean in and press my lips there to check for fever. "We don't want you to make anyone else sick. It's best for you to rest up, snuggle Rocky, and then you'll be good to go on Tuesday."

"Okay."

He's not arguing too hard, which tells me he still doesn't feel fantastic. Keeping him out of school is the right move.

"How about this? Because you were awesome at Nana and Papa's house this week, and you can't go to school tomorrow, I'll reinstate your privileges a day early."

"Really?" His little face lights up with hope. "Can I have them now?"

"You can," I confirm. "I'll go pull them out of my secret hiding place, and you can play video games if you want."

"I *so* want. Thanks, Mom."

I wink at him, then fist bump Max as I pass by him on my way to the master. Alex isn't allowed in my bedroom when I'm not with him, but that doesn't mean that I don't hide the things I take away, just in case.

I have a chest in my closet that I bury under folded sweaters. I move the clothes and open the chest, then pull out Alex's gaming system, games, and his iPad, and replace the sweaters before walking back out to the living room.

Max is on the couch with Alex now, under the blanket, watching the end of *Harry Potter*. I hook up the system and pass the iPad to Alex, but rather than starting it up, he sets it aside to finish his movie.

Maybe taking the extra electronics away for a few days wasn't a bad thing. We may do *unplugged* days once a week for a while. I want my kid to enjoy playing outside and working with his hands.

I sit in the loveseat across from my men and watch as Max wraps his arm around Alex's shoulders, pulling him into his side. He kisses Alex's head, and Alex rests his arm over Max's middle, settling into him.

I blink at tears that threaten and look over at the TV, but my mind is still on the two people across from me. I love them both more than anything in the world. I love that Alex has taken to Max so well. He trusts him, admires him, and there's no one more deserving of that trust and praise than Max.

I wish that Alex had had the opportunity to have this same relationship with Cary, but that wasn't to be. We're here now, with a man who loves us both and wants to protect and care for us.

I wasn't sure that I'd ever see that day. Certainly not with Max because of our past and because I'd moved on from him.

It's new to depend on someone as a partner, and I'd be lying if I said I wasn't resistant to it at first. Like I told Max the other day, I have to protect myself.

I just had no idea how good it would feel to have someone here with me, to help me, to say *"I've got this for now, go take care of you."*

It's the best feeling I've ever had. Better than falling in love. Better than sex.

It's security I've never had before, and I don't want to ever let it go.

"That was a good movie," Max says when the credits roll. "I can't believe I hadn't seen it before."

"You hadn't?" Alex asks with wide eyes. "How is that possible?"

"I don't know. Are the others this good?"

"Oh my gosh, they're the best. Let's have a marathon. We have them all, right, Mom?"

"We do, but I thought you wanted to play your games?"

Alex shrugs. "I can play tomorrow, I guess, after the movies are over."

I share a surprised look with Max. "That's true."

"So, can we?"

"I don't see why not. But first, we need to have a talk."

I turn the TV off and sit again, my elbows on

my knees.

"Oh, man," Alex says. "Nothing good ever comes from that."

Max laughs. "That's exactly what your mom would say."

Alex grins. "I know."

"What do you want to talk about, Wills?" Max asks, his eyes smiling at me.

"Skiing."

"Well, that's my cue to go," Max says as he stands, but I put my hand out, stopping him.

"No, I really want you to stay. We're in this together, remember?"

"I've been in trouble for that already."

"You're not in trouble now," I reply with a laugh. "No one is in trouble."

"Okay, then," Max says as he takes his place on the couch again. "Go on."

"I want to talk about the lessons you've been asking for," I say, addressing Alex directly, and see the hope fill his brown eyes.

"Really?" he asks.

"We're just talking about it right now," I clarify. "I need you to be patient with me, Bubba, because this is something that truly scares the hell out of me."

"It's just that it's so fun," Alex says as he walks over to me and sits next to me. "And I'll always be really careful."

"I know." I kiss his cheek and then his forehead. "Did you have fun with Max?"

"It was the best day of my whole life," he says so earnestly that it tugs at my heart.

I look over to find Max watching us, his face solemn.

"What do you think?" I ask him.

He takes a deep breath and lets it out slowly. "I understand why it scares you. It can be a dangerous sport, but if he's taught by the right people, and always follows the rules and wears his gear, he'll be safe."

"I would do those things," Alex says, nodding with enthusiasm.

"Jacob has some incredible instructors," Max adds. "I hate to break it to you, buddy, but ski season is almost over for this winter."

"Oh." Alex deflates next to me. "That sucks."

He's disappointed, but I'm elated. This gives me a good nine months before I have to think about it again.

"I think there's only one more weekend left," Max continues. "But now we know it's not out of the question for your mom."

"Yeah, that's awesome." Alex leans into me. "What made you change your mind?"

"I can see that you enjoyed it," I reply, thinking it over. "I talked with Nana about it, and she gave me a new perspective on it, too."

"Interesting," Max says.

"I'll tell you about it sometime."

He nods, and I glance down at a smiling Alex. "Now that we've decided that skiing is back on the table for next year, do you want to watch more *Harry Potter*?"

"I just have one question," Alex says.

"What's that?"

"Will you go skiing with us?"

I glance at Max, who's leaning forward, waiting for my answer.

"No," I reply with a laugh. "But I'll go hang out at the lodge and wait for you."

"Okay," Alex says. "Let's watch *Harry Potter*."

***

"I haven't played Pac-Man in years," Max says as he joins me at our table at O'Donnel's. It's Wednesday night, and Alex has the next two days off school, so we invited Pierce to come out for pizza with us before we take Alex to spend one more night with Jean and Dan before they leave for Arizona.

"I can't believe it still works," I say, watching Alex and Pierce take turns on the game. "Alex is good at it."

"He's smart, Wills. And I'm not just saying that because I'm biased. He's highly intelligent. Alex says he struggles with math, but once he grasps the concept, he runs with it. I'm excited to see what he does with all that brainpower."

"I am, too," I admit. "But it's okay if he's a little boy for a while longer. He's growing up so fast."

"I notice his attitude has been better since our week away. Even with being sick."

"I've noticed the same," I reply. "It's been nice to have my sweet boy back for a while."

"Look what the cat dragged in," Max says with a grin, looking at someone behind me. I turn to see Christian and Jenna, along with Nina, walking through the door.

"Oh my gosh! You have to join us," I say, jumping up to give Jenna and Nina a hug. "Tell me you're not taking it to go."

"We're not now," Christian says with a laugh. I flag down the waitress and let her know we're moving to a bigger table, and once we're settled in, I nudge Jenna with my elbow.

"I haven't talked to you in forever."

"You were off on a romantic getaway, and then Alex was sick," she reminds me. "But please tell me we're on for yoga tomorrow."

"I wouldn't miss it," I reply. "Nina, why don't you join us for yoga? You'd love Fallon."

"I think I will," Nina says with a smile. "What are you guys up to?"

"Getting out of the house," Max says with a laugh. "What about you?"

"Well," Jenna says, looking at Christian. He gives her a nod, and she looks like she's about to burst with something. "We're getting married."

"We know," I remind her, pointing at her ring. "We've known for weeks now. Did you hit your head?"

"No," Jenna says, giggling. "We're getting married *this weekend.*" She whispers the last few words, and I stare at her, sure I've misheard her.

"Uh, Jen?"

"Yeah?"

"We haven't planned."

She shrugs a shoulder. "I've planned everything I need to."

Nina glances around the room nervously, probably making sure no one is listening. Christian's had several curious looks since he walked in. I guess that's what happens when you're the most famous actor in the world.

I check on Alex and Pierce, but they're still playing their game, oblivious to the conversation happening at the table.

"Were you going to tell us?" Max asks quietly. He looks irritated, his brows drawn together in a frown.

"I was going to call tonight," Jenna admits.

"I don't love talking about this here," Nina

says.

"There's no one here," Christian says, looking around. "And the two women in the back corner can't hear us. Just tell them, babe."

"Saturday," Jenna whispers, "at the property in the park."

"You're going to snowshoe in your wedding dress?" I ask quietly. "It's damn cold out there."

"No," she says with a smile. "I've talked to the park and got permission to plow the road, just this once. No snowshoeing for it. But, yes, I am wearing a pretty dress. And before you ask, we're only inviting the people at this table, Hannah and Brad, and Jacob and Grace. That's it."

"Wow," I whisper. "What about your parents?"

She shrugs a shoulder but doesn't answer, and that means something's up with that and she doesn't want to say.

I'll figure it out later.

"What time?" Max asks.

"We say our vows at four, just in time for the sunset. The photos will be ridiculous. And then we'll have a small reception at the Lodge on the lake."

"Not Jacob's lodge?" I ask, surprised. We usually have most of our events there.

"Not this time," Jenna says. "I want a lake view."

"I have a lake house," Max reminds her.

"I didn't want to ask," she admits. "Because it's short notice."

Max leans in, looking his sister in the eye. "Anything you want, Jen. Ever. It's never too much. We'll have it at the house, and we'll cater it however you want. Just let me know."

"I love you," Jenna says with tears in her eyes.

"I love you, too," Max says, then reaches for my hand under the table.

"What am I supposed to wear?" I ask.

"Well, I have something for you," Jenna says, reaching into her handbag.

"If it's a dress, it's way too small," I say, making her giggle.

She passes me a card.

I love you, friend. Please be my maid of honor?

"Now you've done it," I say as I swipe at a tear and lean over to kiss her cheek. "Of course. But I still don't know what to wear."

"Something warm," she says with a smile. "No need to be fancy. This isn't about fancy or flashy. It's about love."

"Damn it," Nina mutters, also swiping at tears. "Why do you have to be so damn mushy?"

"I know," I add, nodding. "I can't even with them. They're so romantic."

"So, why do it on the down low?" Max asks.

"Two reasons," Jenna replies. "My brother and

my fiancé are both ridiculously famous, and I don't want a circus. Secondly, I want the marriage. The wedding isn't the priority."

"You've never been one to need pomp and circumstance," I remind everyone. "This actually doesn't surprise me at all, aside from the timing. You could have told me before this. I don't tell your secrets."

"We decided last night," Christian says, smiling down at Jenna. "We're ready."

"Well, then, looks like it'll be a busy weekend," I say with a grin. "Would you rather I ask my mom to keep Alex on Saturday or do you mind if he joins us?"

Jenna frowns. "Alex is part of my family," she says. "He needs to be there."

"Well, I'm just going to spend the night crying," Nina says, reaching for another napkin. "I can't even."

"Yeah, we're mushy," I say with a smile and lean over to hug my best friend. "I'm so happy for you. I want to see pictures of your dress."

"You're going to die," she says, shimmying in her seat. "Like, absolutely die."

"I can't believe you didn't let me help you pick it out. I'm your fashion person."

"I know." She bites her lip. "I saw it online, and I just ordered it. It was a spontaneous decision."

"You ordered a wedding dress without trying it

on?" I ask, appalled.

"Yeah. You know a seamstress, right? In case it doesn't fit?"

"Wait. It's not *here*?"

"It arrives tomorrow."

"That's like *two days* before the wedding."

She nods. "Yeah."

I take a deep breath and laugh. "We've got this. I know people. It's okay. Everything's going to be okay."

"You've broken her," Christian says, laughing hard.

"I'm okay," I reply.

"It's going to be the best day *ever*," Jenna says with confidence.

And I believe her.

CHAPTER EIGHTEEN

Max

"YOU KNOW I LOVE Alex, right?" I walk into my house and toss my keys on the table inside the door, then pull Willa to me, kissing her soundly.

"But?" she asks with a smile.

"But, it's convenient that there are grandparents around who enjoy a sleepover now and then." I pick her up in my arms and head straight for my bedroom. "I'm not at the place where I'm comfortable having sex with him in the house yet."

"And I love *you* for that," she says, cupping my cheek. Every time she says those words, it's a dart to my heart. "We'll get there. Eventually."

"If you weren't a screamer, it wouldn't be an issue."

I grin when she scowls and dump her onto the bed.

"I'm not a screamer."

"I beg to differ," I reply as I peel her jeans down her legs and toss them over my shoulder. "You're a vocal lover."

"I can't help it," she says and reaches for my shirt, tugging it up so she can kiss my stomach. "It's your fault."

"I'm not sorry."

Both of us naked now, I crawl over her, pinning her under me, and nibble her mouth from one corner to the other.

"You're so fucking amazing," I mutter against her lips, making her grin. "You turn me on all the damn time."

"Good. Because it's the same for me." She pulls her knees back in an invitation that I'll never be able to resist, and I slide home, buried balls-deep. "Oh, my God."

"See? Vocal."

She bears down, squeezing me, and I groan in pleasure.

"I'm not the only one."

I bite her lower lip and cup her jaw, continuing to kiss her as I move in a fast rhythm, relishing how damn good she feels.

"You're mine, Willa Elizabeth," I whisper. Her eyes open, and she stares at me with those big, brown eyes that never fail to pull me under her spell. "For now and always, you're mine. I want you to be my wife. I need you with me always, Wills."

She plunges her fingers into my hair, holding me close.

"I *am* yours," she says as I tip my forehead against hers. "And it would be the biggest honor of my life to be your wife."

I stop and gaze down at her, shocked at what just happened.

I proposed.

She said yes.

There was no ring, no fancy dinner or flowers. Just my heart and hers, making the promise of a lifetime.

***

"My car will finally be done on Monday," she announces thirty minutes later. We're sitting in my dark kitchen, eating the leftover pizza. She's wearing my black T-shirt and panties, and her dark hair falls in loose waves around her shoulders.

She's the sexiest fucking thing I've ever seen in my life.

"Okay."

"It's about time."

"It's fine."

She narrows her eyes at me. "It's time for me to have it back. They've been working on it forever."

"Keep the Range Rover," I reply. "I don't use

it, Willa. And you love it."

"I do," she admits with a sigh. "But that's a lot. I can't afford to pay you for it."

I stop eating and narrow my eyes at her. "You're going to be my wife. What's mine is yours anyway."

"No way." She shakes her head. "I'll be signing a prenup."

"Fuck that."

"I will not fuck that. I'll sign a prenup. Max, your financial planners would deck you for even considering *not* having one."

"And I'd fire them."

"This is not an emotional decision. It's business, and it makes sense. If you think you'll get half of Dress It Up, you have another thing coming."

My lips twitch as I watch her take another bite of her pizza. "We'll talk about it later. In the meantime, keep the car. You can sell the other one."

"We'll talk about it later," she says, echoing me. "Did you propose because of all the wedding talk at dinner tonight?"

"No," I reply, shaking my head. "I've wanted to for a long time, but I didn't want to rush things. I just know that I need you. You've owned my heart for all of my adult life, Willa. I need you, and I guess, in that moment, I couldn't hold it in anymore."

She leans on her stool, offering her lips for a kiss. I oblige her, holding onto her neck as I take the kiss deeper, tasting pizza and Willa.

"I'm sorry it wasn't more romantic," I say when I pull away.

"Uh, the man I love proposed in a moment of passion because he couldn't hold it back any longer. I think that's damn romantic."

"You deserve the pomp and circumstance," I reply, echoing the words she used earlier. "The ring and the hoopla."

"I do enjoy some hoopla," she agrees with a grin. "And I won't let you get off easy with a small wedding like Jenna's, but that'll all come in time. The important part is right here, in this kitchen."

"You, me, and pizza?"

"Yep. And Alex, of course."

"Do you think he'll be okay with this?"

She takes a bite, chewing and thinking it over. "I really do. I know it'll be an adjustment, but you've merged into our family so easily already. He goes to you as often as he does me for things like bedtime and help with homework. He loves you."

"I love him, too."

"I know," she says. "If it were any other way, we wouldn't be here."

I nod, and then an idea takes up residence in my mind.

"Question."

"Shoot," she replies.

"Where are we going to live? We can't keep two separate houses forever."

"Good question." She finishes her pizza but tosses the crust back in the box, and I rescue it, eating it in two bites. "It would make sense to live here. Your house is bigger and worth much more than mine."

"But yours is important to you," I point out. "You've lived there a long time, and you've made it a special place for you and Alex."

She nods. "Thank you. I do love the house, and it's the only home Alex has known. The property is beautiful, but so is living on the lake, so we can't go wrong either way as far as that goes."

"I have a suggestion." I push the pizza box away, take Willa's hand in mine, and lead her over to the couch, tugging her down onto my lap. "How would you feel about eventually selling both of our properties and building our dream home, on the lake, together?"

She blinks rapidly, processing the idea. "You would want to sell this house? I thought this was your dream home?"

"It's a great house on the lake, and it's a good investment, but my dream home is the one you and I build together."

She swallows hard. "Would you mind if we lived in the farmhouse until the new one is finished? That way, Alex's world won't be kicked off its axis all at once."

"Of course, I don't mind." I kiss her forehead. "Are *you* sure you're okay with moving out of that house?"

"Yeah. That was a dream with another man. I stayed because it was convenient, and I liked it a lot, but it's time to chase a new dream. Besides, Alex will enjoy planning his own room."

"Own room?" I laugh and kiss her cheek. "Christ, he can have his own wing."

"How big of a house are we talking?"

"Well, this house is about ten thousand square feet, so probably about that, or a little bigger."

"That's right, I'm marrying Mr. Moneybags."

"I love you, Wills."

"I love you, too."

***

"The flowers will be delivered here and at the ceremony site tomorrow morning," Brooke Henderson, the owner of Brooke's Blooms, says Friday morning. She came to my house to meet with me about wedding plans for Jenna and has taken over as a last-minute planner for the whole affair. My sister may not want a showboat of a wedding, but it's going to be a nice one just the same.

"That's great," I reply.

"I've also talked to the restaurant, and they'll be here early in the afternoon to set up for a sit-down dinner for twelve."

"Perfect. What about the cake?"

"Maisey is making it and will deliver it tomorrow, as well. I was thinking we could set it up over here." She leads me over to the window that looks out to the lake. We spend the next twenty minutes going over plans, and when she leaves, I turn to Christian, who's been silent the whole time.

"Are you okay with all of that?"

"It sounds amazing," he replies. "Jenna will be thrilled, and that's all that matters."

"Listen." I tuck my hands into my pockets. "I know that I was pretty hard on you in the beginning. But I want you to know that I like you. I respect you. And if you hurt my sister, my brother is the chief of police, I have more money than God himself, and I can make your death look like an accident."

"Awesome." He smiles and doesn't back down a bit.

Fuck, I like him.

"Now that that's settled," I say and reach for my coat. "Let's go ski a couple of runs before the sun goes down."

"That's the best offer I've had all day."

Christian drives us up the mountain, and I call Brad, Jacob, and Noah, telling them to meet us up there.

Jacob and Noah are already there, of course.

"We have to take advantage of the snow before the runs close down on Monday," I say to Jacob as he and Noah, along with Jacob's friend, Sebastian, approach. "Brad's on his way up. He'll catch us on the second run."

"You read my mind," Jacob says. "You remember Sebastian?"

"You bet. Why do I get the feeling I know you?"

Christian snickers beside me. "Because he was in the same *People* magazine issue you were."

I frown, then it hits me. "Shit, you're *Prince* Sebastian."

"We can just keep it at Sebastian for now," he replies with a smile. "It's been nice to have some anonymity."

"I bet," I reply. "It's one of the things I like about Cunningham Falls. There are celebrities roaming about, but the locals don't care."

"How long are you in town for?" Christian asks him as we retrieve our skis from the back of his SUV, then walk to the chairlift.

"I haven't decided," Sebastian replies. "I just got into town about a week ago, and so far, I don't want to leave."

"You'll fall in love with it," Noah warns him, clapping him on the shoulder. "Okay, boys, which run should we take first?"

"Let's do chair five first, then meet with Brad and take it from there," I suggest.

The snow is perfect, light powder. It's cold, but there's no wind, so the skiing conditions are ideal.

Once Brad joins us, we spend the next three hours on the slopes, laughing and enjoying each other. Because it's so late in the season, most of the tourists have gone home, giving us plenty of room to play.

I know that Willa doesn't love skiing, but it's so freeing. It's like flying, and it's always been something I crave. No matter how long I was away from home, I always longed to be back here, flying down the mountain.

"This mountain is bloody brilliant," Sebastian says, breathing hard as he pulls his goggles off. "I've skied in the Alps, all over the world, really, and I'd say this ranks at the top."

"It's a hidden gem," Jacob says. "Not as hidden as it used to be."

"And that's both good and bad for the locals," Noah replies with a shrug. "For many people, it's driven the property taxes so high they can't afford to live here."

"And yet, it's also provided a lot of jobs and opportunities that weren't here before," I add. "It's a catch-22."

"Either way, I love to ski on it," Sebastian replies. "And I'd like to take you all out for dinner, if you're free."

"I am," Noah says with a grin.

"Unfortunately for you, but fortunate for me

because I'm a lucky bastard, I'd best get home to Grace. She's been with the baby all day, every day. Now that the season is winding down, I need to be home more."

"I need to head home, too," Brad says. "But thanks for the offer. I'll see you tomorrow, guys."

"Christian?"

"I'm getting married tomorrow," he reminds us. "If I don't go home to help Jenna, she might murder me in my sleep."

"What about you, Max?"

I start to answer, but before I can, everything goes black.

CHAPTER NINETEEN

Willa

"YOU GOT SO LUCKY," I say, looking up at Jenna. I'm squatting in front of her, pinning the hemline of her wedding dress. "I can't believe it's just the hem that needs to be done. Otherwise, it fits like a glove."

We're in my shop, in the back room that I have set up for private fittings and parties. Sometimes, girls like to shop privately, and I'm more than happy to accommodate them. So, I have a beautiful, antique, three-way mirror with a pedestal set up in the middle of the space, and chairs in the corners.

"It's so beautiful," Jenna breathes. It's just the two of us on this Friday afternoon, fussing over her dress. "And I can't believe how much Max and Nina are doing to help get ready. Did you know he commissioned Brooke to take over as the planner?"

"Yes, he told me last night," I mutter around the pins between my lips. "He's excited for you."

"It's *so fun.* And exactly what I wanted. I know that Christian's fans are hoping for a big spread in a magazine, but we're private people."

"And it's none of their damn business," I reply, moving to the other side of her. "I have news."

"What's that?"

"Max asked me to marry him."

The hem is yanked out of my hands as Jenna spins around and pulls me to my feet, hugging me with all her might.

"Holy shit! Oh my God, Willa! You're going to be my sister for *real.*"

I hold on tight, pure joy surging through my body.

"Why didn't you call me when he asked?"

"We were having sex at the time," I say with a laugh.

"Um, we need to change your proposal story. That can't go in *People* magazine." She leans back to look me in the eyes. "I'm so happy for you. So, *so* happy."

"I'm happy for both of us. Who would have thought?"

She turns with her arm around my shoulders, and we look at our reflections in the mirror. Jenna in her amazing off-the-shoulder, white wedding dress, and me in my deep purple winter dress. Her fair features, and my dark.

We're yin and yang.

And the closest of friends.

"Who would have thought, indeed," she says with a grin and glances at my hand. "No ring?"

"It was spontaneous," I say with a shrug. "And you know he'll pick something up for me sooner or later."

"I can't wait to see it," she says with a grin. "It's going to be ridiculously amazing."

"I hope he doesn't spend what I paid for my house."

"Don't be silly," she scoffs. "It'll be way more than that."

I choke on a laugh and have to take a swig of water. "What am I getting myself into?"

"The ride of your life, my friend. Now, I feel so much better seeing the dress on. Thank God it ran true to size."

"I won't have to outsource the hemming," I reply. "I can do it myself. It'll only take about an hour."

"That long for a hem?"

"It's not just the outskirt, it's all of the layers underneath, as well. And you want those layers because they'll keep you warm out there in the boonies."

"Oh, let me show you the wrap I bought," she says, gathering the skirt and walking to a bag on the chair in the corner. "It's going to be warm *and* beautiful."

"Oh, Jenna," I breathe, taking the white, faux fur wrap from her and rubbing it reverently. "This is stunning. And so soft."

I wrap it around her shoulders and step back, grinning.

"You look like a fairy princess," I say, getting choked up. "And Christian is going to lose his shit when he sees you."

"That's the plan," she says with a laugh. "Are we finished pinning?"

"Yep, I have it marked. You can put your clothes back on." I tug the zipper down in back so she can easily step out of it, and she hurries into the changing room, pulls the curtain closed, and quickly changes into her jeans and sweater.

Just as she's stepping into her snow boots, Melanie pokes her head around the corner.

"Willa?"

"Hi, Mel. We're almost done here. Do you need me?"

"No, I just wanted to make sure everyone was dressed. Brad Hull is here to see you."

"Must be wedding stuff," Jenna says with a grin as Brad walks around the corner, but I can see by the look on his face that it's not wedding stuff.

It's bad.

"What's going on?" I ask.

"Well, Willa, we went skiing."

I have to sit in the chair before my legs give out from under me.

"Who? Was Alex there?" I know that my son is with my mom today, but maybe Max picked him up. Wouldn't he call me?"

"No, Max, Christian, and some of the other guys. We went up this afternoon for a few runs, but Max was hurt."

"No." I shake my head, focusing on the floor. "No. He's not hurt."

"Jesus, how badly?" I hear Jenna ask as my heart beats out of my chest, and my hands shake. I can't breathe. Is it hot in here? Why is it so hot in here?

"We don't know," Brad says grimly. "The ambulance took him to the hospital, and I came here to get you two."

No. This can *not* be happening again. Not again. Not to Max.

"Come on, Willa, we have to go."

"I can't go," I reply and jump up, putting my pins and scissors away. "I have too much to do. I have to hem Jenna's dress, and I have to see to the store."

"Willa," Brad says, but I shake my head.

"I'm sorry, I can't go."

"Hey." Jenna grabs my shoulders in her hands and makes me look her in the eye. "You have got to get your shit together, Willa, because Max needs us at the hospital."

Tears swim in my eyes. "I can't," I whisper. "I can't do this again."

"Oh, baby," she says, but doesn't lose the firm grip on my shoulders. "You can, and you will. Your fiancé needs you right now."

"Fiancé?" Brad asks in confusion.

"He asked her last night," Jenna says, not looking away from me.

"Bastard didn't say anything," he mutters. "The car's running, girls."

"Come on," she says, taking my hand and leading me out to the car, parked just outside the back door of the shop. She guides me into the passenger seat, and when both Jenna and Brad are seated, we zoom off toward the hospital, Brad flipping on the siren.

"You have a siren in your personal car?" I ask.

He doesn't answer. He's too intent on getting to the hospital, and I just feel *numb*.

What will I do if Max is gone? How can this be happening to me again?

***

"Concussion," the doctor says grimly. I'm sitting next to Max, who has a bandage wrapped around his head. He's sleeping. He hasn't woken up since the accident. "He'll be here for a couple of days while we monitor. I don't like that he's still unconscious."

The doctor says more things, but I tune him out, staring at Max as I hold his hand and will him to wake up.

Wake up.

Jenna and Brad are both with me, and all the others are in the waiting room, anxious to hear how Max is doing.

"I'll go tell the others," Brad says. "Can I bring you two anything?"

I don't reply, but I hear Jenna say, "Just some water, please."

The door closes behind Brad, and Jenna sits across from me, taking his other hand.

"He's ruined your wedding," I whisper.

"Christian's already called the vendors, and they're on standby for an alternate date," she says easily. "That's the thing about a simple wedding. It can be changed."

"I'm sorry," I say and lay my forehead against the back of Max's hand.

"What are you sorry for?"

"That I'm so weak." It's barely a whisper. "I'm scared out of my fucking mind."

"Hey, that's normal under any circumstances, but with your past? Willa, of course, you're terrified. But you heard the doctor, he has a concussion, and he's going to be okay."

I swallow hard as Max shifts on the bed and briefly opens his eyes, looking around the room as if he's drunk out of his mind.

"There she is," he says, but falls back to sleep.

"The doctor said he's been doing that off and on," Jenna says.

Brad comes back with water. "Mom and Dad are here."

"They were going to surprise you all tomorrow at the wedding," Jenna says with a shrug. "So it's good they came today. They should come in."

They do. I'm hugged and fussed over. I don't really pay too much attention to what's said. I can't breathe well. I'm having the longest anxiety attack on record.

Finally, everyone leaves for the night, and I'm left alone with Max, still sitting in the same chair by his side, willing him to wake up.

The sun set hours ago. Jenna checked in with my mom to give her an update on Max and to make sure Alex was okay.

The only thing I've been able to think all day long is, *I can't do this.*

There's shuffling behind me, and I turn to find Cary's dad, Dan, standing in the doorway.

"Hey," I say, standing and stepping into the hallway with him.

"I just wanted to stop by to see how he's do-ing." The strain on his face is heartbreaking. This has to be like deja vu for him, too.

"He's going to be okay." I let the tears fall now,

splashing on my cheeks. "But I'm so damn scared."

"Hey there," he says, pulling me in for a hug. "This is different from before."

"I guess." I swallow. "I just don't think I can do this. He asked me to marry him, Dan, but how can I do that when I'll be terrified every day that something like this will happen again and he'll leave me?"

I back away and wipe at my cheeks.

"Willa—"

"I know, it sounds ridiculous, but I can't help it. I would rather end things on my terms than have him ripped out of my life."

"You listen to me, little girl," he says firmly, catching my attention. "I've never known you to be a selfish coward."

I flinch at the words.

"If you love him and you want to be with him, you march back in there, and you stick with him. Through this and any other hard times that come along. Because I promise you, there will be hard times."

"He could die."

"We all could," he says. "Or he could live to be a hundred and four. Do you want to miss out on all of those good years? Whether it's two days or into your nineties, you love him. That's how it works. You don't get to run away."

I wipe my eyes and take a deep breath.

"No one except for Jenna and Brad knows that he asked me to marry him."

"I'm happy for you," Dan says kindly. "You're good for each other. He's great with Alex."

"But Cary—"

"Is gone," he says. "As much as I wish I could change it, Cary is gone, my dear. You *have* to live your life."

"You and Jean have both said that to me." I sigh again. "I just wish I could shake the guilt."

"You have to," he replies. "Or it will fester and steal your joy. Don't let it do that. Are you going to be okay here? Do you need anything?"

"No." I glance inside the door to find Max still sleeping. "I'm okay."

"Just call if there's anything I can do."

With another hug, Dan leaves, and I return to Max's side. I'm not a coward. And I'm *not* selfish.

I'm scared.

With Max's hand in mine, I lean on the bed, just to rest for a few minutes.

"It wasn't his fault," Cary says. He's sitting across from me in my living room, but it's not my living room. It's the way it used to be when Cary and I were first married.

"Whose?"

"Max's. It wasn't his fault today, and it wasn't his fault back when I died."

I frown, and everything comes back to me. The funeral. The flowers. Max. Alex. Jenna's dress, and Brad telling me that Max was hurt.

All of it.

"I've been angry with you," I admit, watching his face, soaking him in. He's still twenty-three, and handsome. So young.

"I know. I was stupid that day, Wills. I shouldn't have skied that run, but I was showboating, showing off for Max because he'd been gone so long, and I was trying to show him that I was cool. I got the girl, I was having a baby, and I was still cool."

"You hurt him. Hurt us."

"I was a selfish idiot," he replies with a grin. *"And I paid for it."*

"We all paid for it."

I want to slap him. And I want to hug him. So, I do. I walk to him and climb onto his lap, hugging him close. But it feels so foreign, from a time long ago.

"Doesn't fit anymore," he says as I pull back. *"And it shouldn't."*

"I carry a lot of guilt," I admit. *"I know you're gone, and your dad is right, I need to move on. I deserve that. But—"*

"No buts," he interrupts. *"And stop it with the guilt, Wills. You haven't done anything wrong. Do you want my blessing?"*

I shrug.

"Well, you have it. Max is my best friend, and if he's the one for you, I want you to be with him. Live your life, Wills. Enjoy it."

"Alex loves him, too."

Cary grins. "That kid is a firecracker."

"He's got so much of you in him."

"Just don't let him forget me," he says and looks to his left as if someone just walked up.

"Who's there?"

"It's nothing," he says. "I want you and Alex to be happy. That's all I've ever wanted. You're doing a great job at the mom thing, just like I knew you would."

"You would have been a good dad."

"Maybe," he says with a nod. "But you know who I know is going to be an awesome dad? Max."

"Yeah." I nod, thinking about the man who's gone above and beyond to make sure that Alex and I are safe, taken care of, and loved. "Yeah, he's going to be a great father. If the mountain doesn't kill him."

"The mountain didn't kill me," he stresses. "I did that myself by being dumb. And today, Max was just standing at the bottom of a run, minding his own business. Some stupid tourist who didn't know what they were doing ran smack into him, knocking him out cold."

"You saw that?"

"I see a lot."

I stare at him, mortified that he might see Max and me when we—

"No," he says with a laugh. "I don't see that."

"Well, thank goodness. Am I going to see you again?"

"Someday," he replies and leans over to kiss my cheek. "But not for a long time. Go enjoy your life, Wills. Marry Max, have more babies. Just don't forget me."

"Never."

CHAPTER TWENTY

Max

"I *WANT YOU TO be happy."*

I'm standing in a living room, watching Cary and Willa have a conversation. She's sitting in his lap, which I don't like at all. Cary turns and glances at me for a moment, then looks back at Willa. She asks him who's there, but he brushes it off, and they continue their conversation.

They're talking about me.

I try to speak, but they can't hear me. Or Cary's ignoring me.

Finally, Cary kisses her cheek, and she disappears into thin air. Cary stands, walking to me.

"This was our living room."

"That's where I recognize it from," I say.

"I guess you heard that. It was all my fault, man. All of it. But the way it all went down, well, it's held Willa back from being able to live guilt-

free. To heal from the grief."

"And now?"

"She's going to be okay," he says with a smile. "The skiing still scares her."

"I'm not the biggest fan now either."

He laughs but shakes his head. "You'll get back up there. That's how it works, remember?"

He's echoing the words I said to Alex that day on the sledding hill.

"He loves you," he says, his face sobering.

"I love him, too. Both of them. Cary, I asked Willa to marry me."

His face lights up in a bright smile.

"Good for you. You got the girl, after all."

"It was never a game for me," I remind him.

"I know that. I guess my sense of humor isn't as good in the afterlife. You've been having some monster dreams, man. You need to let go of all the guilt and anger. You didn't kill me. You love Willa and Alex, and they love you back. Enjoy them."

"Thank you. For your blessing. I know it means a lot to Willa, and it means the world to me."

"I love you. All of you. Take care of them for me, yeah?"

"Yeah."

"All I ask is that you don't let Alex forget about me. Tell him about me. Max, you knew me better than anyone. Share that with him."

"I promise."

He reaches out to shake my hand, and I pull him in for a fierce hug.

"I'm going to leave you be," he says. "No more dreams. I'll see you later. Much later. But you might see little hints that I'm around from time to time."

"Good. Because I'll miss you, man."

He nods and smiles. "Go. Willa needs you."

My head is fucking killing me. I feel like I got hit by a freight train.

Someone's holding my hand. I open my eyes to find Willa next to me, but she's sitting, not lying in our bed. I'm in a hospital room.

The last thing I remember was skiing, and now…I'm here?

Shit.

Willa opens her eyes and immediately looks up at me. "You're awake?"

"Hey." My head is going to split open. "Whisper, okay? Head hurts."

"I'm sorry." Her eyes fill with tears. "Max, I dreamed about him. About Cary."

"I did, too."

She frowns. "Was he looking at you?"

"Yes."

"I couldn't see you."

"I know. But I could see you, and I could hear you, too."

She swallows and kisses my hand. "He said goodbye, and he asked me to be happy. To live my life, with you, and enjoy it."

I want to hold her so fucking badly, so I find the bed control and raise my head more, then pat the bed next to me. "Come here."

She readily complies, gingerly sitting next to me where she can still look at me.

"After you left, he said the same to me," I say and reach up to brush a piece of hair off her cheek. "He gave us his blessing, Wills."

"Yeah."

"He just asked that we don't let Alex forget him."

"We won't," she promises. "I have a confession."

"Okay."

"I almost left. Today, after the accident. I almost ran away from you because the thought of losing you tore me up inside."

"If you left, I'd follow you and find you."

"Stalker."

"No, I love you, and I know you love me, too. You don't get to leave me, Wills."

"Back at you. No more scaring me like this."

"Deal."

"Are you going to ski again?"

"Oh, yeah." I grin at her and squeeze her hand. "And maybe, one day, I'll get you up there, too. There's nothing to be afraid of."

She nods and then purses her lips as if she's thinking about something serious.

"What's going on in that beautiful head of yours?"

"You're an intimidating man, Max. What can I possibly give to you that you don't already have?"

I smile. "A daughter."

***

"I can't believe that Jenna and Christian got married on a Wednesday," Alex says. "I mean, who does that?"

"They wanted to be unique," Willa says.

"It's cool that I got to stay home from school so I could go to the wedding."

The reception is over, and everyone has left, including the crew that came in to clean up.

My sister and Christian got married today, only four days late, exactly the way Jenna wanted. At the property in the park, with a small reception after at my lake house. We're going to stay here tonight and move back to the farmhouse permanently tomorrow.

"Bubba, we have something to talk to you about," Willa says as she joins us in the living room, bringing us each a cup of hot cocoa. "How would you feel about Max and me getting married?"

Alex's head whips around, and he pins me with a hopeful stare. "Did you ask her?"

"I did. I'm sorry, I should have asked you first if it was okay, but I got carried away."

"Do we have to get rid of Rocky?"

I scowl. "Of course, not. I love Rocky."

"Focus," Willa says with a sigh. "We need to know how you feel about this."

"I think it's good," he says, staring at his cocoa. "I have lots of questions, though."

"Ask all of them," I say and rub his shoulder. "We're happy to answer them."

"Are we gonna move in here?"

"No," Willa says, and Alex's face falls in disappointment. "Wait, do you want to live here?"

"There's a whole movie theater," he reminds her.

"We plan to build a new house," I reply. "One that you can help design your own space in."

"That's cool," he says, then gets super serious. "I want to ask Max a question, but I don't want to make Mom sad."

"You're fine, Bubba. What is it?"

He looks up at me nervously. "After the wedding, can I call you Dad? Since you'll be Mom's husband and stuff?"

I take a deep breath, my eyes finding Willa's.

She gives me a nod, and I pull Alex into my arms, giving him a big hug.

"Is that what you want?" I ask him.

"Well, yeah. I mean, I know I have another dad, but I just think it would be cool to have *you* as my dad."

He knows how to reach in and tear my heart to smithereens. I cup his face and smile at him. "Yes, you can call me Dad. Nothing could make me happier than that."

"Cool." He smiles at his mom, then scowls when he sees her tears. "See? I didn't want to make you sad."

"You didn't." She laughs and swipes at the wetness on her cheeks. "These are tears of happiness. I think that calling Max Dad is really great."

"I have one more question," Alex says.

"Okay," Willa says.

"Can we have a baby?"

***

"Is our wedding going to be like Aunt Jenna and Uncle Christian's?" Alex asks the next night as he sets the table for dinner. He's started using *aunt* and *uncle* when referring to my siblings and their spouses now that we're getting married. Alex might be the most excited of all of us.

"No way," Willa says, shaking her head as she sets mashed potatoes on the table. "I do *not* want to get married in the snow."

"Where would you like to get married?" I ask her, burying my nose in her neck.

"Maybe the beach?" she says. "I know a great resort in California."

"You don't want to get married here, with all of your friends and family?" Alex asks with a frown.

"We'll fly them all there, if that's what your mom wants," I reply. "But there's still time to talk about it."

"In the meantime," Willa says as we sit down, "we are doing something new tonight."

"Pot roast is new?" Alex asks. The kid makes me smile.

"Listen to me, please," Willa says, and Alex makes the motion of zipping his lips shut and throwing away the key. "From here on out, Thursday nights are date nights. Dad date nights."

"Every Thursday," I continue when Alex frowns, "we will talk about your dad, and you can ask about him, too. We'll tell stories, look at pictures, and eat some of his favorite foods. Sometimes, we'll have others over who knew him, and sometimes, like tonight, it'll just be us."

"Wow," Alex says. "That's kind of cool."

"Pot roast with mashed potatoes was his favorite home-cooked meal," Willa says as she dishes up Alex's plate. "With extra gravy."

"I want extra gravy," Alex says. "What other foods did he like?"

"He loved pizza with Canadian bacon and pineapple," I say, thinking about it.

"I don't like that," Alex says. "What else?"

"Remember that burger place that used to be just outside of town?" Willa asks. "He *loved* that place."

"One time, when we were in high school, Cary and I went to that burger joint, and he hit on the waitress."

"I didn't know that," Willa says.

"Well, she turned him down flat. But as we were leaving, she gave me her number and asked me to give it to him. She was shy."

"Did he call her?" Alex asks with a grin.

"He did. And they went out on a date. I think it was his very first date ever, but he was so nervous, he threw up on his way there. He had to stand her up and go home to clean his car."

"That's horrible," Willa says, her face horrified. "Poor Cary."

"He ended up doing all right," I remind her with a raised brow, and she laughs with a nod.

"That's true."

"What else did you used to do with my dad?" Alex asks as he shoves mashed potatoes into his mouth, then slips a piece of meat down to Rocky.

"When we were really young, like about your age, we would go camping."

"Alone?" Alex's eyes widen in surprise.

"Yeah, just the two of us. My dad would drive us up the road a bit from their old house where there was a campground, and we'd pitch a tent and roast hot dogs on the fire that one of the other campers would make for us."

"Good God, don't even *think* about doing that," Willa says to Alex, rubbing her fingers over her forehead. "Maybe this was a bad idea."

"No way, this is awesome," Alex says with a laugh. "Can you take me camping?"

"I don't see why not. Oh, this one time, we were down at the river fishing, and your dad caught a fish that was at least five pounds."

"No way," Alex says with excitement. "My dad liked to fish?"

"It was his favorite thing," I confirm. "And he was good at it, too. I always thought it was a little boring, honestly."

"I'd like to fish."

"Maybe Papa will take you this summer," Willa says. "Papa taught your dad, you know."

"Papa's good at lots of things," Alex says with a nod. "He'll totally take me. He said he'd teach me how to play baseball, too."

"Your dad was an all-state baseball player," Willa says. "Max and I used to go to every single one of his games to cheer him on."

"Wow," Alex says. "That's really cool. Does he

have trophies?"

"I'm sure he did," I say with a frown and look over to Willa. "Do you know if Jean and Dan kept any of his things from school?"

"I think so," she says with a thoughtful nod. "I'll ask them, and then when they come up for the summer, maybe they'll show them to you, Alex."

"That would be awesome. I think Thursdays are going to be my new favorite. It's even better than Taco Tuesday. Tell me more."

"Well, remember when I said your dad loved to fish? This one time…"

I settle in, eating and telling stories about my best friend to my son, watching his face light up in excitement at hearing about the man who gave him life.

And when I gaze at Willa and see the love reflected back at me, I realize that the worst moment in my life gave me the best ones. That as we move on from grief and guilt, we're blessed with the gift of joy and love.

And I don't think I can ever thank Cary enough for that.

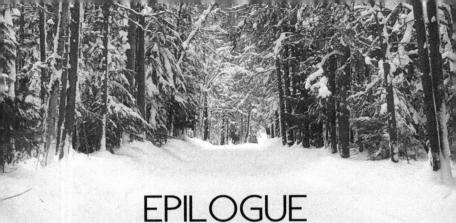

EPILOGUE

Willa

"**T**HIS IS A TRADITION?" Alex asks as we set up camping chairs in the snow at Cary's grave. "With root beer and everything?"

"I usually bring real beer, but neither you nor your mom can drink that, so, root beer it is," Max says with a wink, pops the top off one bottle of the soda, and sets it on top of the tombstone. I lay the red roses at the base of it. "Your dad gets the first one."

Max opens three more and passes them to us, and then we all sit down as if we're settling in for a long chat.

Because we are.

"Hi, Dad," Alex begins. The train whistle blows, making me smile and look over at Max, who's also grinning. "I guess this is my first time here."

It's been a year since the day I walked up to this spot and found Max here. A year since my world changed forever.

"I think you're old enough to come," I reply and take a sip of my root beer. It's cold, but we're all nicely bundled up, with toe and hand warmers stuffed into our socks and gloves. "You can talk to him, you know."

"Yeah," Alex says, staring at his bottle. "We have lots to tell you, Dad. First of all, Mom and Max got married last year. I call him Dad now, and I hope that doesn't make you mad."

The train whistle blows again, and I smile softly. Cary's here, and he's talking to Alex.

"The wedding was in California, which I thought was kinda weird at first, but it turned out really great."

Alex spends the next fifteen minutes giving Cary a play-by-play of the past year.

"Oh, and I got a dog. His name is Rocky. I wanted to bring him to show you 'cause he's the best dog there is, but Mom said it's too cold today, so he's at home. I'll bring him in the summer so you can meet him.

"My best friend, Pierce, got a dog, too. But Rocky's better. When I told Pierce that, he said I was full of shit."

My head whips up in shock. "Alexander Cary Monroe-Hull. Watch your mouth."

He grins and giggles. He loves to say shocking things so I use his full name. He was thrilled when Max presented him with adoption papers at our wedding, hyphenating his last name.

"His dad would have laughed his ass off at that," Max whispers to me, and I narrow my eyes at my husband.

"You're not helping."

"We get to move into our new house this summer," Alex continues, chatting as if he were actually sitting with his dad. "And I'm excited because I have a whole suite of rooms, with a game room and everything. Mom's gonna let me decorate it. Oh! And Mom has news, too. Go ahead, Mom."

"You want me to tell him?"

"Yeah." He takes a swig of his root beer and grins.

"Well, we're going to have a baby." I cover my belly with my hands over my coat and rub a circle. "We're only halfway there, and she'll probably come when it's time to move into the house because nothing's ever easy, but we're excited."

"The baby's suite is the same exact size as mine," Alex says. "But first, she'll be in a room by Mom and Dad's room that they'll make into a sitting room later."

He sounds so grown-up, talking about babies and house plans.

"When did you grow up?" I ask him. "Where's my baby?"

"In your belly." He giggles. "I'm a big kid, Mom."

"That you are. Do you have anything else to talk about?"

"No, I think that about covers it," Alex says.

"Then I guess we'd better go," I reply. "If you want to get some skiing in this afternoon, we need to get a move on."

"I wish you could ski with us," Alex says.

"It's not that I'm afraid, Alex. Remember?"

No, I've let go of the fear.

"I know. You have to protect Bailey."

"That's right."

"I'm going to hang back for a second," Max says and kisses me on the cheek. "I'll be right behind you."

"Is everything okay?"

"Everything is perfect. I just need to thank him."

I frown, but then understanding dawns.

"He already knows, my love. But I understand."

I turn and follow Alex to the car, with Bailey turning circles in my belly. I don't know what Max just said to Cary, but the train whistle blows behind me.

SOARING

WITH *Fallon*

A BIG SKY NOVEL

NEW YORK TIMES BEST SELLING AUTHOR

KRISTEN PROBY

CHAPTER ONE

Fallon

"**N**AMASTE."

"Namaste," my class repeats. Some of them jump up immediately to get on with their days, and some sit quietly for a few more minutes.

Summer yoga is my favorite. I get to teach classes every morning at the Lodge on the Lake, for tourists and locals alike. Some days we're overflowing with newcomers, and some days like today, it's mostly familiar faces.

The sun rises early in this part of the world during the summer months, so a start time of seven a.m. is perfect to get the blood moving through our veins.

"Sorry I came rushing in late, Fallon," Nina Wolfe says with a smile. She's rolling her mat. "I can't believe I over slept."

"No worries," I reply. "It happens to all of us. I'm just glad you made it."

She sighs and walks over to me, her mat slung over her shoulder. Nina is a pretty blonde woman, with an athletic body and a happy smile. She moved to Cunningham Falls, Montana just a few months ago to be closer to her brother, Christian.

Who happens to be Christian Wolfe, the hottest Hollywood actor in the world.

Of course, he's married to another client of mine, Jenna.

"How long have you lived here, Fallon?" Nina asks.

"Oh goodness, it must be almost two years now." I blink rapidly, realizing that this is the longest I've stayed in one place in more than five years. "Wow, time flies."

"Was it hard for you to feel like you fit in? To make friends? I mean, I have Christian and Jenna, and I have acquaintances of course, but—"

"I get it," I say with a nod. "Small town life is different. There's not a lot of people here, and it feels like there are a lot of cliques."

"Yes," she says with a relieved nod. "And most everyone I know is originally from here, so they have that network in place. I just wanted to make sure I wasn't going crazy."

"You're not," I assure her and pat her shoulder. "And it does get easier."

"Why don't we go get some drinks or coffee or something sometime," she asks. "I've been coming to your class for months. We're friends."

"Sure." I reach into my bag and pull out a card. "My cell is on here. Just text me and we'll set it up."

"Awesome." Nina grins and takes a step back. "I also might have some professional things to discuss with you. Pick your brain."

"I'm always happy to have my brain plucked." I wink and sling my bag over my shoulder, walking toward my car. "Have a good day, Nina."

"See you!"

I climb in my Jeep and drive toward my house, which is just a couple miles away. Sometimes I walk to class, but I was running late this morning myself.

And I admit, I like the feel of the sun beating on me, the wind blowing through the Jeep as I drive.

After the long Montana winter, summer is just what the doctor ordered.

I've just stepped through my front door when my phone rings. I grin as I answer.

"Hey there."

"Hi yourself." Claire, my friend from back home, yawns in my ear. "Whatcha doing?"

"Just got home from class," I reply as I brew some tea. "It sounds like you just woke up."

"I did." I can hear the smile in her voice.

"Does that mean someone just left?"

"He left awhile ago," she says. "And I don't

think I'll be seeing him again."

"What's wrong with this one?" I carry my tea out to my back patio and sit at my outdoor dining table. This spot is what sold me on renting this house. The trees and bushes are in bloom, making it feel like a magical garden.

"He moans weird," she says, making me laugh. "Like an old man bending over to put on his socks."

"Not sexy," I agree.

"Too bad, too. He had a nice body. Ah well, there are about a billion more out there."

"With nice bodies? Maybe not a billion."

"You're right. Are you dating a hot cowboy yet?"

I grin and trace the Drips & Sips logo on my mug. "No. It's a small town, Claire. Not a lot to choose from."

"So when are you going to move on to the next place? Or come home?"

I sigh, thinking it over. I don't think I'll ever move back to Chicago. Now that my grandma's gone, I don't have any family there, and Claire is my only tie to the city. I've been roaming around the country, living in my bucket list towns for the past five-plus years.

"I like it here," I reply.

"You've been there longer than the others."

"I know. I just realized this morning that it's been almost two years. I like the community. I'm making friends."

Claire scoffs in my ear.

"What was that for?"

"Fallon McCarthy, you don't make *friends*. You make acquaintances. And even then, getting to know you isn't easy."

"I know," I murmur. That's the way it's always been, my whole life. I'm an introvert. I enjoy my own company more than I like being with others. "People exhaust me."

"Maybe that's why you're better in a small town," she says. "Fewer people."

"That's definitely a plus," I agree. "What are you doing today?"

"I'm going in to work for a bit."

"On a Saturday?"

"Hey, you worked today."

"For an hour. I don't have any other classes today."

"Well, I have some accounts to work on. What are you going to do with the rest of your day?"

"I think I'll go on a short hike," I reply. "It's a beautiful day today."

"Like, on the treadmill?" she asks. "A simulated hike?"

"No, city girl, a *real* hike. In the woods. On a path."

"Do you, like, have hiking boots?"

I smile and tip back in my chair, enjoying my friend. "I have hiking shoes. They're not boots."

"Huh. Well, whatever floats your boat, my friend. Have a good day."

"You, too."

I hang up, go inside to rinse my mug and put on the hiking shoes that will need to be replaced soon, and drive across town to my favorite hiking trail.

One of the things I like best about Cunningham Falls is all of the outdoor activities here. There are miles and miles of hiking trails that the city keeps groomed and safe for hikers. Last week when I came to walk on this particular trail, it was closed due to mountain lion activity.

That gave me pause.

But I carry bear spray, and the only animal I've ever seen on the trail is deer.

Half-way up to the lookout point, I get a text from Nina.

Breakfast tomorrow? 9:00 at Ed's?

I grin and type a quick reply.

Sure, see you then.

Claire's right, I don't easily make friends. I wouldn't even consider Claire my *best* friend. She's a close friend. But the sad thing is, she's probably the best friend I have.

I just don't tell her everything.

I don't even have a bunch of baggage in my

past that would cause my lack of trust in others. No one has betrayed me. Or bullied me.

It's just my nature to hold back. To be the observer and soak everything in.

And because of that, I am sensitive to moods and emotions, and that's exhausting.

So instead, I've made a habit of being a loner. It suits me fine.

But having breakfast with a new friend sounds fun, too. Maybe I'm just evolving as a person. I'm only thirty-two. A person can change.

I come around a corner and shift to the side of the trail so a runner can zoom past me. He nods in thanks and keeps going.

Nice ass, I think to myself with a grin.

I set off again, about to come over the ridge to the overlook. It's a great place to sit and breathe, watching the lake and the boats floating on it, not to mention the gorgeous Blacktail Mountain above it.

But a rustling in the bushes catches my attention. I reach for my bear spray, just in case, but then pause and squint, trying to see what's going on.

"It's a bird," I mutter, stepping closer. A white head pops up and I gasp. "A bald eagle. Hi there, sweetie. Are you hurt?"

One wing is flapping, but the other wing isn't moving at all.

It's hurt.

"Crap, I don't know what to do about this. I'm

not ready."

I look up and down the trail, but there's no one close by. The runner is long gone.

So, I pull my phone out of my pocket and call Claire.

"Did you get eaten by a tiger?" she asks.

"There are no tigers in North America, Claire. But I did find an injured eagle. I don't know what to do?"

"Why did you call me?" she asks.

"Because *I don't know what to do.* Tell me what to do."

"Call animal control?"

I frown, watching as the poor thing struggles. "What are they going to do? Fine it?"

"I live in Chicago, Fallon. I don't know. Call 911. Call the sheriff. Call *anyone* but me."

"Thanks a lot." I hang up and take a deep breath. "Who do I call for you?"

A veterinarian!

I Google vet offices in Cunningham Falls and call the first one on the list.

"I'm on the Bear Mountain trail, just outside of town, and I found an injured eagle. What do I do?"

"Oh, you'll want to call Spread Your Wings," the receptionist says. "They'll come help you."

"Thanks." I hang up, not at all sure of what Spread Your Wings is, but a phone number comes up when I Google it, so I call.

"This is Noah."

"Uh, hi, my name is Fallon. I just found an injured eagle." I repeat my location.

"Don't move," he says briskly. "I'm coming right now. How far up the trail are you?"

"I'm maybe twenty yards from the top."

"Of course you are," he says. "Looks like I'm going for a hike. I'll be there in less than thirty minutes. Can you stay there?"

"I'll wait," I confirm, and he hangs up. "Well, looks like help's coming. Don't worry, they'll get you all fixed up."

I'm talking to an eagle.

I sit on a stump and don't take my eyes off the bird. He's watching me as well.

"I'm friendly," I say. "And I won't hurt you. How long have you been here?"

He squaks, making me smile.

"Maybe you don't speak English. I'll be quiet. But I'm here with you."

I take two long, deep breaths, trying to calm my heart. If I'm upset, the bird will be upset. I don't know how I know that, I just do.

It's like when you're trying to calm an upset baby.

Not that I've ever had a baby.

"Now I'm being ridiculous," I mutter.

It feels like three hours later when I hear some-one hurrying up the trail.

"Fallon?"

"Over here," I call and stand, waving my hands. "We're over here."

A man appears, carrying a huge animal carrier. He's hardly winded, and I know he had to practi-cally run up this mountain to get here so quickly.

"I'm Noah," he says. "Where is it?"

I point to the pushes, where the eagle had fi-nally calmed down.

"He's there. One of his wings isn't moving."

Noah approaches the bird, and before I know it, he's secured something over its eyes and managed to put it in the carrier.

"Wow, you've done that a time or two."

"Or fifty," he says with a smile. "I'll get him down to the sanctuary and have a look. Thanks for calling it in."

"Of course," I reply and watch as he walks away, hurrying down the trail. "Bye."

I look around, not sure what to do next. So I finish my hike to the overlook and watch the boats, take in the sounds of the woods around me, and then start back down to the Jeep.

What a weird day.

***

"You totally saved an eagle's life," Nina says before taking a bite of her pancake.

"No, I called Noah, and he saved it."

"He wouldn't have done that if you hadn't called. Noah's a nice guy."

"Do you know him?" I ask, trying to sound casual. "I'd never met him."

"Sure, he's good friends with Max Hull, and the rest of the Hull family, I guess. I've met him a few times." She stops chewing and grins at me. "He's hot, isn't he?"

"Is he?" I sip my tea. "I hadn't noticed."

"Uh huh. Sure. And I'm a coal miner's daughter." She leans in. "He's single."

"How nice for him."

She smirks. "And you're interested."

"How did we get on this subject?"

"You should go see him," she continues. "And check in on your eagle."

I blink at her, thinking about it. "Why would I do that?"

"Because you're an attractive, single woman, and Noah's single and you should go flirt with him. What will it hurt?"

I frown. "I never said I wanted to flirt with him."

"Fallon, we may not know each other well, but I know the look of a woman who's interested in a man. And when you said Noah's name, you got that look."

"Okay, so he's attractive," I reply. *Yeah, try smoking hot in all fifty states.* "That doesn't mean I need to go flirt with him."

"Are you dating someone else?"

"No."

A slow smile spreads over her lips and I feel myself start to give in.

"Fine. I'll go check on the eagle. But only because I'm concerned."

"Sure. That works. Okay, now that I've solved your love life issues—"

"I don't have love life issues."

"—let's talk about something else just as fun. I'm starting a business in town, and I'd like to talk to you about some opportunities."

"I have a full time gig between the Lodge and the studio downtown."

"Well, just hear me out, and then you can give it some thought."

I nod, and Nina continues, telling me all about the business she's start with two of her friends from California. A business to help busy women.

"Basically, there may be times that I would call to book an in-home yoga session. We could work around your schedule, of course."

"Interesting," I reply with a nod. "It's something to think about, for sure."

"That's what I was hoping you'd say. Saffron and Lindsey will be here in a couple of weeks, and we're hoping to have things up and going next month."

"Thank you for thinking of me," I reply.

"You're the best in town," Nina says with a wink. "And we want the best. So think it over, and we can get together any time to fine tune things."

"Thank you."

Once I leave Nina, I make my way over to Drips & Sips for my favorite tea. I have my own lemon oil with me to flavor it, ignoring the looks I get from the women tourists waiting for their lattes, and then I climb in my Jeep and drive out to the Wild Wings bird Sanctuary.

I looked up directions this morning, before my breakfast with Nina.

Something just told me I should go say hello.

And I usually listen to that *something*.

The sanctuary is out of town, in the middle of nowhere. Which makes sense because the animals are wild, and they need plenty of space.

There's a farmhouse across the pasture from the industrial buildings. And the sign over the driveway says *Spread Your Wings*.

This is the place.

I park and walk into an office area that's currently deserted.

"I wonder if I should have called ahead," I mutter out loud.

"Nah, there's always someone bustling about." I startle at the voice and turn to find Noah standing behind me with a grin. "Fallon, right?"

"Yeah." I reach out to shake his hand, and feel the warmth climb all the way up to my shoulder. His hand is calloused and large, engulfing my small one. "And you're Noah."

"Guilty," he says. "Did you come to check on your eagle?"

And to check you out.

"I did," I say. "I know it probably seems weird, but—"

"Not weird at all. Follow me."

We walk outside and down a long, paved side-walk that meanders through several buildings.

"I wasn't expecting it to be this big," I say.

"That's what *she* said," he replies with a grin, and I can't help but laugh out loud. "Sorry, couldn't resist. We've grown a lot in the past few years."

He leads me into a big building and down a row of cages, then stops and gestures.

"Well, hi there," I croon. "How is he?"

"He has a broken wing," Noah says with a sigh. "We can't tell what caused it. But I think that with about six weeks of healing time, he should be good to be released back into the wild."

"Really? That's amazing. What if he can't live

in the wild again?"

"He'll stay here, with us, and we'll use him for education. He'll have a cushy life here, but I suspect he'll be leaving us. He's a healthy guy."

We're quiet as I watch the bird. He's looking at me, as if he recognizes me. There's a splint on his wing.

"I'm so glad I found you," I murmur.

"Me too," Noah says, and smiles when I look over at him. "The bird, not me."

"How long have you been doing this?"

"Most of my life, but I started the sanctuary eight years ago. I have a masters in zoology from Colorado State."

"Wow. And you came back to Cunningham Falls?"

He grins, and I feel it in my gut. Goodness, Noah King has a great smile.

"I have roots here," he says. "It's home."

I nod and look back at the eagle. "He's gorgeous."

"You can visit him anytime you like."

I start to decline, but reconsider. "You know, I might just do that."

"Good." He clears his throat. "I hate to do this in front of our feathered friend, because I'll be embarrassed if this goes badly, but can I interest you in dinner?"

"Tonight?"

"Anytime you like," he replies with that easy smile. "Tonight. Tomorrow. Right now."

"It's not even noon."

"It's five o'clock somewhere."

I laugh and look down at my feet, then shrug. "Sure. A girl has to eat, right?"

"Exactly. May I see your phone?"

I hand it over, and he punches in some numbers.

"I just texted myself. If you text me with your address, I'll pick you up at seven."

"It's a deal."

I say goodbye to the eagle, and Noah escorts me back to my Jeep.

"I'll see you tonight, Fallon."

"See you."

I drive away, Noah's voice tickling my mind. The way he says my name is like a promise. Like he likes the sound of it on his tongue.

Fallon.

It's not like me to accept a date invitation, but there's something about Noah King that I like very much. What will one dinner hurt?

ABOUT KRISTEN PROBY

Kristen was born and raised in a small resort town in her beloved Montana. In her mid-twenties, she decided to stretch her wings and move to the Pacific Northwest, where she made her home for more than a dozen years.

During that time, Kristen wrote many romance novels and joined organizations such as RWA and other small writing groups. She spent countless hours in workshops, and more mornings than she can count up before the dawn so she could write before going to work. She submitted many manuscripts to agents and editors alike, but was always told no. In the summer of 2012, the self-publishing scene was new and thriving, and Kristen had one goal: to publish just one book. It was something she longed to cross off of her bucket list.

Not only did she publish one book, she's since published more than thirty titles, many of which have hit the USA Today, New York Times and Wall Street Journal Bestsellers lists. She continues to self publish, best known for her With Me In Seattle and Boudreaux series, and is also proud to work with William Morrow, a division of HarperCollins, with the Fusion and Romancing Manhattan Series.

Kristen and her husband, John, make their home in her hometown of Whitefish, Montana with their adorable pug and two cats.

Website

www.kristenproby.com

Facebook

www.facebook.com/BooksByKristenProby

Twitter

twitter.com/Handbagjunkie

Goodreads

goodreads.com/author/show/6550037.Kristen_Proby

Other Books by Kristen Proby

The Big Sky Series

Charming Hannah
Kissing Jenna
Waiting for Willa - Coming Soon

Kristen Proby's Crossover Collection – A Big Sky Novel

Soaring with Fallon
*Wicked Force: A Wicked Horse Vegas/Big Sky
Novella by Sawyer Bennett*
*All Stars Fall: A Seaside Pictures/Big Sky Novella
by Rachel Van Dyken*
*Hold On: A Play On/Big Sky Novella by Saman-
tha Young*
*Worth Fighting For: A Warrior Fight Club/Big
Sky Novella by Laura Kaye*
*Crazy Imperfect Love: A Dirty Dicks/Big Sky No-
vella by K.L. Grayson*
*Nothing Without You: A Forever Yours/Big Sky
Novella by Monica Murphy*

The Fusion Series

Listen To Me
Close To You
Blush For Me
The Beauty of Us
Savor You

The Boudreaux Series

Easy Love
Easy Charm
Easy Melody
Easy Kisses
Easy Magic
Easy Fortune
Easy Nights

The With Me In Seattle Series

Come Away With Me
Under the Mistletoe With Me
Fight With Me
Play With Me
Rock With Me
Safe With Me
Tied With Me
Breathe With Me
Forever With Me

The Love Under the Big Sky Series

Loving Cara
Seducing Lauren
Falling For Jillian
Saving Grace

From 1001 Dark Nights

Easy With You
Easy For Keeps
No Reservations
Tempting Brooke